Readers love *Heart Unseen*
by ANDREW GREY

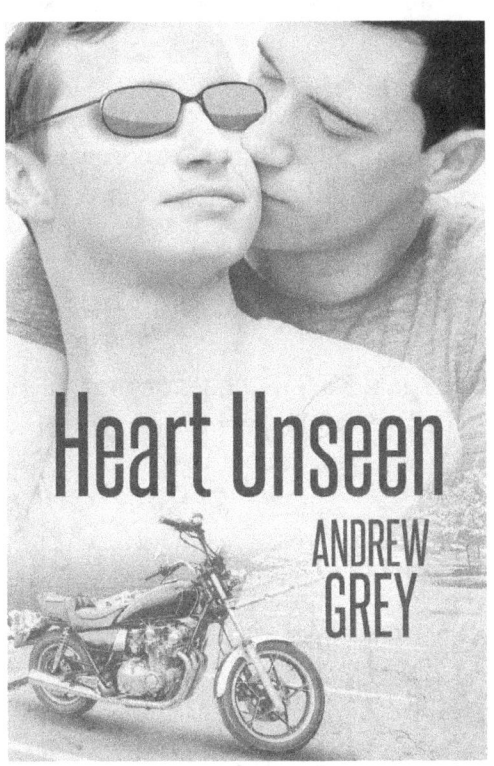

"I have no hesitation in recommending *Heart Unseen* to all m/m romance lovers and Andrew Grey fans!! Andrew is going from strength to strength and with this book he has got a winner!"
—Love Bytes

"Overall, this is a beautiful story... Highly recommended."
—On Top Down Under

"Of course, this is Andrew Grey, so they get their HEA, leaving this reviewer feeling warm and fuzzy in the area of my heart and with a smile on my face."
—Hearts on Fire Reviews

More praise for
ANDREW GREY

Fire and Fog

"Andrew Grey really knows how to give his target audience what
they want. Everything about this book works for me."

—Love Bytes

"It's getting harder to pick a favorite from the Carlisle Cops series.
With this sixth installment, Andrew Grey combines suspense,
investigative skills, and a good mix of characters."

—The Novel Approach

Growing His Dream

"Once again Mr. Grey does an amazing job of bringing the reader
into the lives of the people he is writing about."

—Paranormal Romance Guild

"Andrew Grey works his magic to bring a smile to my face and a
warm and fuzzy feeling to my heart."

—Hearts on Fire Reviews

Setting the Hook

"Andrew Grey's books are a must-read in the m/m romance genre.
He simply knows how to write, and gives the reader stories about
everyday people living everyday lives."

—Two Chicks Obsessed

"This is a romance that is sweet, with a little bit of angst and family
interference, but it is one you will enjoy tremendously. I can't
recommend it highly enough. Enjoy!"

—Happy Ever After, *USA Today*

By ANDREW GREY

Published by DREAMSPINNER PRESS
www.dreamspinnerpress.com

Published by DREAMSPINNER PRESS
www.dreamspinnerpress.com

Heart Unheard

ANDREW GREY

Published by

DREAMSPINNER PRESS

5032 Capital Circle SW, Suite 2, PMB# 279, Tallahassee, FL 32305-7886 USA
www.dreamspinnerpress.com

Heart Unheard
© 2017 Andrew Grey.

Cover Art
© 2017 L.C. Chase.
http://www.lcchase.com
Cover content is for illustrative purposes only and any person depicted on the cover is a model.

ISBN: 978-1-64080-151-6
Digital ISBN: 978-1-64080-152-3
Library of Congress Control Number: 2017953208
Published November 2017
v. 1.0

Printed in the United States of America
∞
This paper meets the requirements of
ANSI/NISO Z39.48-1992 (Permanence of Paper).

To Cheryl Hoffman and all my fans. You're the reason I write, and you provide me with my source of creativity.

CHAPTER 1

BRENT BERKHEIMER sat in his small office and peered out the window. He sighed and craned his head, looking for Scott, then groaned softly. He needed to stop doing that. He'd already done it a dozen times today, and dammit, he needed to get his mind where it should be. The bay where the young mechanic worked was the closest one to his office, and Brent liked to watch him in action. Brent was the boss, though, so getting involved wasn't a good idea.

However, he had just talked it over with Trevor Michaelson, the owner and his boss, who told him that as long as he kept things professional at work and didn't allow any drama or tension to creep into the workplace, he wasn't going to tell him no.

"Just be careful," Trevor said, sitting across from Brent in his office. "I've seen the way the two of you look at each other, and I know we've talked about things."

Brent nodded. He agreed—which was why he'd stayed away for almost two years. Scott Spearman had just turned twenty when Brent had taken over for the previous guy, who had stolen a great deal of money and nearly gotten Trevor into irreversible financial difficulty. So for the last two years, Brent had just watched, hoping his infatuation would die away.

It hadn't.

Brent wandered out to the shop floor as Scott grunted and humphed from under the hood of the Firebird. He walked to the other side, sticking his head underneath to take a look. Cars weren't his forte. Brent wasn't a mechanic by trade. Rather, he was a manager and kept the business humming and everyone working at their best.

"What's the trouble?" He leaned forward a little more.

Scott raised his gaze, and Brent swallowed hard as warmth flowed into Scott's wide eyes. Brent watched his throat work before turning away. This was such a bad idea. "This nut won't loosen." Scott lowered his gaze and went back to work, but his hands didn't seem to be moving and he glanced upward again.

Heat built inside Brent, and he nodded without breaking eye contact, wondering what those eyes and incredible lips would look like in the height of passion. Shit, he needed to keep thoughts like that at bay. They were working, dammit. "Have you tried backing the seal? Tap it on the side with the wrench." It was a trick he'd seen some of the other guys try.

Scott released the wrench and gave the bolt a couple taps. He seemed skeptical, but when he turned it this time, the dang thing moved a little and then more. "Awesome."

"How much longer before you'll be done?" Brent asked, but Scott kept his head down until he got the bolt off. This time when he raised his gaze, his cheeks were flushed and red.

"A few minutes now." Scott nearly dropped the bolt, and Brent pulled back from under the hood of the car, still watching Scott as he walked back around to the office and went inside, tugging a few times at the collar of his shirt to let some air in and cool the sweat that had formed under it.

He met Trevor's gaze for a second and snatched some papers off his desk to have something to take his mind off the sweet drink of walking temptation on the other side of the glass.

His heart still beat faster twenty minutes later while he was discussing the state of business with Trevor and doing his best not to look out the window. It was best to leave things as they were.

"I'm heading out," Scott said as he stuck his head in the office door, his shaggy black hair falling almost to his eyes. He was a little on the lanky side, but with deep brown eyes that reminded Brent of hot chocolate on a cold winter night. He had pouty lips that burst into a bright smile at the drop of a hat. "I finished everything, and I called all the owners for them to pick up."

"Do you have something fun planned?" Trevor asked.

"I need to get home and stuff. Lee and I are both off tomorrow, and we're going swimming. It's been so hot and the water is great, so I'm going to take him. His mom is going to drive us." He was so excited, Brent grinned. Then Scott turned to him and his lips curled just a bit, his pupils growing bigger as his gaze heated slightly. Brent's temperature rose and he smiled in return.

"You have fun." Brent couldn't look away. The intensity in Scott's eyes was the world's best candy, and he wanted a bite. Brent was already sweating, and all Scott had done was poke his head in to say goodbye. Staying away from him was getting more and more difficult.

"We will." Scott left, and for a second, Brent pictured him in his bathing suit, one of those Speedos, dripping with water as he rose out of the waves James Bond–style.

Trevor stood and peered outside before closing the door. "Jesus. I think I need a shower." He sat back down and fanned himself. "Man, it's warm in here. You need to make up your mind and do it fast. Either tell him how you feel and then the two of you figure this shit out, or walk away. The energy between you is enough to light the block for a month. If you keep this up, you're going to sizzle the paint off the walls."

Brent nodded. "I know. I keep hoping that things will work themselves out and that he'll tell me what he wants or something. Scott is young and has his whole life ahead of him. He doesn't need a washed-up guy a decade older tying him down."

Trevor shook his head. "Sometimes I wonder if you aren't as blind as James. At least he has an excuse. Scott just sent you a message with exactly what he wants. Hell, he couldn't have been clearer if he'd contracted Western Union to send you a damn telegram."

"I know. But… I'm not like you and Dean. You have enough confidence to approach anyone, and Dean is still working his way through the entire gay male population of Milwaukee. He's got the slut thing down pat." Brent grinned. "Sometimes I think he should give classes."

"He's free and making the most of it. Dumbfuck Chuck really did a number on him, and I don't think he's going to change his ways until he gets whatever he has going on out of his system." Trevor paused. "Nice change of subject. Look, my dad would tell you to shit or get off the pot. And that's my advice too. Do something instead of standing around my business, eye-fucking each other until the end of time." Trevor fanned himself once again, then pulled his ringing phone out of his pocket. "James, I'm leaving the garage and heading home… no, we'll eat in." His voice grew deeper, and Brent left the office to give him some privacy. The last thing he wanted to hear was Trevor and James making plans for their certain-to-be-spectacular evening.

Last summer Trevor had decided to take James boating, and the two of them, along with Dean and Brent, had rented a cabin in Northern Wisconsin. They had a great time… until that first night when James proved to have one hell of a set of lungs on him. Brent wondered if they'd had to add some additional soundproofing to the house to comply with noise ordinances.

"Is there anything else you need from me?" Trevor asked as he came out of the office, closing the door.

"I don't think so. We're booked solid for the next week, with half the appointments for the week after booked as well. Things are going well and everyone is getting along, at least for now. Lee is doing really great and seems happy. So be sure to pass that on to James."

"I know. James still sees him on an occasional basis, and apparently all Lee talks about is his time here and the fact that he has a real job doing things he loves." Trevor grinned. "When I brought him here, I didn't expect things to work out as well as they have." He checked his watch. "I should be going."

A car turned off Brown Deer Road, steam pouring from under the hood. It was clearly overheating. The driver pulled to a stop and turned off the engine. A girl of about seventeen got out, staring at the cloud, and began to shake. "Can you help me? I was on my way home and it started doing this. I didn't know what to do and then I saw your sign, and...." She shifted from foot to foot. "It's my dad's car and he's going to kill me."

"I'm Brent, and this is Trevor." Brent approached her slowly. "You did the right thing. We'll let the car cool down, and then we can take a look and see what's wrong." He smiled, and she turned to him and then to Trevor, her eyes lighting up. Of course she'd respond to Mr. Gorgeous.

"We have some coffee and water inside." He led her inside to the waiting area. "Just relax and have a seat. We'll do what we can." Trevor went inside and returned with a few tools. The cloud of steam was becoming a trickle as the heat dissipated. Trevor got the hood unlatched and lifted. More steam billowed out, and then it gradually came to a stop. "There it is, just a loose hose."

Brent came over and nodded. He saw the issue as well. "We'll need to let it cool some more. I'll get a fresh clamp, and we can get this fixed in a jiffy." He went to get the part and brought it back, along with the tools they'd need. After waiting a little longer and letting the air flow around the engine, they were able to get the clamp switched out and to add coolant. Then Brent started the engine and let it run. No more steam.

"Here you go, miss," he said when he brought her the keys. "It's all fixed. Your dad should have the car looked at and checked over thoroughly, but you should be okay to get home."

"How much is it?" she asked, clearly nervous. "I mean, I think I have a ten, but...."

"It's all right. Just get home safely." Brent smiled, and she thanked him half a dozen times before getting in her car. She started it and rolled down the window to thank them again before driving off. "You should get home," Brent said to Trevor. "James is probably wondering where you are."

Trevor already had his phone out and was texting madly, using a voice app.

Brent sighed and went back into the office to get things ready to close up. There wasn't anything more he could do today, but he wasn't interested in going home. He checked his watch again and went through his mental list to make sure everything he needed to do had been completed.

Trevor came in behind him. "Do you need my help?"

"Nope. I'll take care of everything and drop off the deposit on my way home." Brent walked over to the bays, lowered the doors, and started turning off the lights. By the time he got back to his office, Trevor had his things together and was ready to head out.

Car tires crunched on the drive, pulling to a stop right outside, and Brent checked his appointment files. "I don't have anyone bringing in any cars." He stood to look out the window. "It's Jane, Lee's mother." He left Trevor in the office and quickly walked over to where she was parked. "Is there something wrong?" He leaned on the door as the window slid down. Lee sat in the passenger seat, tears leaking from his unseeing eyes.

Lee and Scott were partners and inseparable at work. Lee had been one of James's students at the school for the blind and he loved cars, so James had suggested Lee come to the garage. He and Scott hit it off instantly. They were a great pair, both gifted with engines. And with Lee's almost bat-like hearing, he could diagnose some problems quicker than anyone else in the shop.

"Lee, I wasn't expecting you."

Jane handed Lee a tissue and then turned to Brent. "We just got a call from Scott's mother. He… he was in an accident on the way home. She said she was on her way to the hospital, and Lee asked me to take him to make sure Scott is okay."

"Mom, he was injured. She said so," Lee said as he wiped his eyes. "We have to get there." Lee's voice broke, and Brent's knees buckled. The only reason he didn't end up on the ground was because he used the car to prop himself up.

Trevor came up behind him. "You go do what you can, and tell Scott's family that we're all pulling for him and to keep us informed. Let us know if there is anything that any of us can do."

"I will," Lee said, and his mother turned to them, clearly worried.

"It's bad," she mouthed, sending a shiver through Brent's gut. "We'll ask his family to call. I'm sure it's too early to know anything just yet." She nodded and raised the window.

Brent stepped back so she could pull away, then stood in the center of the drive as she turned onto the street. He blinked and managed to stay upright.

"It's going to be okay," Trevor said. Brent had almost forgotten he was there.

"You don't know that." Brent went inside and sat at his desk once more, not caring if Trevor followed him. There was nothing he could do. He had dithered and told himself to wait, letting himself doubt and vacillate for so long that now the Fates had acted.

"Scott is young and strong, and that's going to make all the difference." Trevor pulled him into a hug. "Just be strong too. I know you have it in you."

That was well and good, but Brent wasn't sure if he had it in him. The Fates had a way of shitting all over him, and this seemed like another of those times.

"We've been friends for a long time," Trevor said.

Brent nodded.

"You're the strong one. You got me through the heartache with Chase when I didn't think I'd ever be able to bounce back. You know, I used to hug you just because you made me feel safe."

Brent forced a smile. He knew he had an image to uphold. In their group, Trevor was gorgeous, the one who could get anyone, but now he was off the market. Dean was impulsive and tended to be wild, at least in the last few years. Brent was the strong, reliable, sensible one of the group. But he didn't feel very sensible right now. Yeah, he was concerned about Scott because he worked with him, but the tightening in Brent's gut and the waves of regret that broke over him again and again reminded him he felt so much more for him. Brent knew he was being completely stupid. He'd never approached Scott, even though they had teased and being in the same room with him sent his pulse racing. To Brent, that wasn't strength, but pure cowardice.

"Dammit," Brent spat and returned to his closing checklist. "Go on home to James, and you two have a good night. You've kept him waiting long enough. I'll call Scott's family in a few hours, find out how he is, and let you know." There was nothing anyone could do right now.

"If you're sure…."

"I am." Brent needed to be alone for a while. "I'll see you soon." He had to keep his mind on the task at hand. He completed prepping the money and checks for the night's deposit, and once he was done, he locked everything up and went to his car. He dropped the bag in the night deposit drop on his way home. He'd brought the number for Scott's emergency contact with him and dialed it through his car's voice commands, then waited for it to connect.

"This is Brent from the garage. How is he?" he asked once the call connected.

What he got as an answer was a sniffle and then tears from Scott's mother, he presumed. There was a shuffling sound before a male voice spoke. "This is Reggie Spearman, Scott's dad."

"Do you know what happened?" Brent pulled to a stop at a gas station and brushed his eyes with the back of his hand. He couldn't drive and have this conversation. It was affecting him too damn much. As soon as he switched off the engine, his hands shook and he clamped his eyes closed.

Mr. Spearman choked up, making Brent regret asking. He should have kept his mouth shut. "He was stopped at a light and seemed to have slipped his seat belt off his shoulder. A car ran into him from behind, and he went upward and hit his head on the windshield and his chest on the steering column. He has a number of injuries, and they're prepping him for surgery."

"Is there anything I can do?"

"Not right now. He hasn't been conscious since they brought him in."

"How did you know he'd been in an accident?"

"The car registered that it had been in an accident, and when the service didn't get an answer, they called authorities and then us. It's the plan we put him on for safety. Help was there right away." He spoke very softly, so Brent turned up the volume.

"Please let me know if there is any change. All of us are concerned and sending him our most positive thoughts." What the hell else could he say? That he hoped Scott was going to be okay so he could get a second chance? He'd clearly missed his first, and if he were lucky, he might get another. Fuck it all. He understood what they meant about a brave man dying one death while a coward dies many. He wished now that he'd had the guts to tell Scott…. He pulled his head out of his own thoughts as Scott's father continued.

"If he recovers, we don't know what sort of therapy he's going to need, and…." His voice cracked.

"One thing at a time," Brent said. "Let's get him through the surgery, and then we'll all go from there." God, he had no idea what was going to happen. "Please call me once you know anything. Any time. It doesn't matter." He had to know.

"Of course. I have your number in my phone now." Scott's father was having a hard time talking, so Brent said goodbye to let him go.

He sat in his car as it heated up in the summer sun, breathing and trying not to beat himself up over and over again. There was nothing he could do now but wait.

Brent backed out of the parking space and continued the drive home. His phone rang as he pulled into his apartment building. "Hey, Dean," he answered, seeing his name on the in-dash display.

"What happened? You sound messed up."

"Scott, one of the guys at the garage, was in an accident. It's pretty serious," he said, keeping his voice steady.

"Is that the guy you've had a thing for and not done anything about?" Dean asked in his "I told you so" tone. At least it was the one Brent's mother used when that was her unspoken message. "What? You've been talking about him for years now, I swear. Whenever we get together, you slip something that Scott did into the conversation."

"Yes, that's him." Brent gripped the steering wheel, his defenses rising.

"I'm sorry, dude. That's pretty tough." And just like that, Dean proved he could be human and had a heart. "What do you want me to do?"

"There's nothing anyone can do. Not right now." Brent opened the car door, which switched the call back to his phone. "I guess I have to hope he makes it through this."

"Yeah. That's tough," Dean repeated. "I was calling to see if you want to go out, but that probably isn't a good idea. So how about I swing by the liquor store, pick up something good, and we can tie one on? I'll be at your place in an hour or less."

Dean hung up before Brent could refuse. He groaned and called Dean right back.

"Don't you dare tell me you want to be alone or some such rubbish. I know what it's like to feel completely stupid. Remember Dumbfuck? The shithead is getting married to the guy he cheated on me with. So I'm on my way." He hung up, and Brent knew it was no use calling him back again. Brent couldn't argue that having some company would be a bad thing. When Dean got something in his bonnet, there was no stopping him.

Brent climbed the stairs to his second-floor, two-bedroom unit and went inside. It was serviceable but nothing special. He got out the munchies he had in the cupboards, ran the vacuum, and got the dishwasher running after he got the dishes out of the sink. He didn't worry about the furniture, which was relatively plain. Dean had been here before, so there was no need to try to put his best foot forward or to keep up appearances.

The doorbell rang. Brent answered it and ushered Dean and his bags inside.

"Let's get started." Dean hurried right into the kitchen, grabbed two glasses, added some ice, and returned to the living room with a bottle of Jack, which he plopped down on the table. He unscrewed the cap, poured the glasses half full, and handed one to Brent. "Now that we have what we need…." Dean gulped from his glass, and Brent did the same.

"Does Scott?" He stared at the amber liquid in the glass. "He may not survive at all, and God, if he does…." He coughed and swallowed around the lump in his throat. "He's going to be in so much pain and…." The liquor sloshed in the glass from his shaking hand. The thought of Scott hurting made it hard to breathe for a few seconds.

"Brent…." Dean leaned forward.

"What do you want me to tell you? I was such a fucking coward…." Brent drank, the whiskey burning as it went down his throat. Then the warmth spread out inside and he drank again, needing that feeling desperately. "A gutless wonder, okay? I worked with him for two years, saw him all the time, watching him like some perverted old fart." He emptied the last of his whiskey and poured another. Now that he was getting into this, he might as well get really shit-faced and see if it helped.

"Is that what you did?" Dean ruffled his hair like Brent was a kid. "Come on. He worked for you, so you wanted to keep things professional."

"Fuck that. I thought… think about him all the damn time. I was too afraid to say something in case he turned me down. I'm ten years older than him, and I figured, what the hell would he want me for anyway?" Brent set his glass aside. Suddenly getting drunk and trying to forget everything didn't hold any appeal. "I'm mooning over a guy who was out of my league. We flirted and had fun with each other, but that was all it was. I was… am Scott's boss, and that's the end of it." He huffed. "The rest is me being an idiot."

Dean downed his whiskey and poured some more. "If you're so sure about that, you wouldn't be acting this way." He could be so observant every now and then. "You like him, and somehow you developed feelings for him."

Brent jumped to his feet, waving a hand. "Okay, I did. But none of that matters, and I need to get over this… infatuation. He's in surgery right now, and he isn't going to want me when… if he gets better." He began pacing the room. "I'm acting like a teenager. I need to stop." His head was going in a million directions, and he desperately needed it to settle on something, anything.

Dean set his glass on the coffee table. "Fuck it all. You know I was pissed and a bit depressed because Dumbfuck was getting married and the asshole is happy. But dammit, I'm more depressed now than I was when I walked through your door." He snatched his glass and drained it. "I hate shit like that." Dean leaned back on the sofa, cradling his glass.

"Let's eat until we puke." Brent opened the bag of Cheetos and passed them to Dean because he knew they were his favorite. Then he opened the chips and went to the refrigerator to grab a couple of beers before flopping on the sofa. He'd had enough whiskey, so he popped a beer open and drank. Brent sighed. "Sometimes I think I'm the stupidest man on earth."

"Why?" Dean's speech was a little slurred, or maybe it was the mouth full of Cheetos. It was hard to tell.

"Because I wasn't gutsy enough just to tell him what I wanted. I know it won't make a difference, not now." Brent drank another sip of beer and then picked up the bag of chips. "I suppose we always regret the things we don't do."

Dean shook his head. "Yeah, I know that. I should have left Chuck long before I did."

"You know, maybe it's time you stop trying to screw every guy in town and find someone special." Brent set his beer on the coffee table, turning toward Dean. "Every time I go to Trevor's and see him and James together, I get so fucking jealous that I want to scream. They have what I want, and I can't ever seem to find it for myself." He crunched another chip. God, now he was sharing his feelings and shit. It must be the whiskey. "Forget I said anything. Okay? It's not that important. Let it go." He turned on the television and found a RuPaul marathon. It gave them something to talk about other than his feelings.

DEAN CONTINUED drinking well into the evening. Brent watched television, and after nursing his second beer, switched to water. He'd had enough, but Dean seemed intent on getting drunk. When he could barely keep his head up, Brent helped him to the spare bedroom, got him some water and aspirin, and put him to bed. Then he went to his bathroom, where he got rid of the beer he'd rented, drank water himself, and then climbed between the sheets.

He'd had enough alcohol to easily fall to sleep but woke, with his legs twisted in the bedding, from a disturbing dream where everyone in his life was just out of reach. A vibration on the nightstand drew his attention. He snatched at it. "This is Brent." His mouth felt like cotton and tasted terrible.

"This is Reggie Spearman, Scott's father. You said I should call."

"Of course," Brent said gently. "I'm glad you did. How is he?" His insides clenched, fearing the worst.

Reggie groaned, and Brent expected that he and Scott's mother were beyond exhausted. "He's come through the surgery and they're sending us home. They said there will be nothing more to learn tonight. They had to pin some bones in his chest, but it was his head that they're most concerned with. They relieved pressure on his brain and stitched up some bad cuts, but they won't know for a while if there is any brain damage. They're hopeful, but the accident was pretty bad."

"Has he woken up at all?"

Reggie sniffed. "No. They're hopeful that when they reduce the drugs in the morning, he'll come around, but they aren't sure. They said…. They…. He could slip into a coma. All they keep telling us is that it will take time and they'll have to see." His emotions seemed so close to the surface, Brent found his rising as well.

"Thank you for calling me. I appreciate it. If there's anything I can do, just say so." Brent swallowed as he tried not to picture Scott lying motionless in a hospital bed.

"Not now."

"I'd like to see him." The thought flashed in his head, and at the late hour, he didn't have his mental filters working to stop it.

"I don't know if they'll allow it, but I'll give your name to the desk. It's only family at this point, but I think I can get an exception. Scott always spoke so highly of you. He loved coming into work every day, and a lot of that was because of you." Reggie sighed once more. "I need to take my wife home so she can get some rest."

"Thank you for calling." Brent ended the call and put his phone back on the nightstand. He closed his eyes, saying for Scott a silent prayer that he remembered from Catholic school. Brent didn't know where it had come from—he hadn't thought about any of that for years—but it came unbidden to his mind, and he recited it as he fell back to sleep.

He woke to the first rays of sun coming through his window. Working at the garage, the days often started early, and he had gotten used to the hours. Brent got up, checked on Dean, who was snoring like a lumberjack, and headed to the kitchen to make some coffee. After that, he called Trevor and explained what Scott's family had told him.

"I want to go up to the hospital to see him, but I don't know if they'll let me in." In the middle of the night, he had made up his mind to at least try to visit Scott.

"Of course. I'll open this morning for you. Do what you have to do," Trevor said, proving once again that he was a great boss and the best friend Brent had ever had.

"Thanks. I need to get Dean out of my guest room before I go."

Trevor chuckled. "What the heck did he do?"

"He came over to keep me company, I guess, and got really drunk. He's been doing that a lot lately." As Brent thought about it, he realized Dean had been drinking excessively for months. "He was drinking Jack like it was nothing."

"Well, take away what he brought and get him up. I'll have a talk with him, and if that doesn't do any good, I'll sic James on him. No one can turn him down for anything." Trevor chuckled. James had a way of getting under everyone's defenses. Part of it was probably the blind thing, but it was also probably that fact that James had a way about him that made everyone want to talk to him. "Did he say why he was drinking so much?"

"Yeah. It seems Dumbfuck Chuck is getting married to the guy he cheated on Dean with. I think it's hit him pretty hard. He needs someone who will care about him, but they're going to have to bring a bazooka to blast through this fuck-everyone-he-can persona Dean's developed." Brent pulled open the refrigerator door and grabbed the orange juice. "Not that I don't care, but it's been two years. He needs to move on."

Trevor scoffed loudly. "That's the pot calling the kettle black."

Brent groaned, knowing Trevor had a point.

"I'm just giving you a hard time. Go see Scott and call me when you find out anything. I'm going to see about taking up a collection of some sort at each garage location. There's certain to be bills that Scott's family isn't going to be able to afford." And that was another reason why Brent and Trevor were good friends. "Call me when you know something."

"I will." Brent hung up, drank his glass of juice, and went to wake Dean, then took a shower and brushed his teeth to get the taste of death out of his mouth.

"Dean, you need to get moving." Brent poured himself a mug of coffee, sipped it, and then poured a second. He figured he could use the aroma as a lure.

"Why did you let me drink so dang much?" Dean shuffled into the room in his wrinkled T-shirt and boxers. The shirt was looser than last summer, and the boxers hung lower on his hips. Dean was incredibly skinny.

Brent handed Dean his coffee. "Have you been eating?"

"Of course I have. Lots and lots of salad." Dean sat down and hung his head. "I need to stop this shit."

Brent rolled his eyes. "Yes, you do. You also need to eat… really eat. And something other than just salad and Cheetos. And drink some water—anything that isn't whiskey or other alcohol." He went into his bedroom and brought back the stand mirror from the top of his dresser. It had been his mother's. Brent plopped it on the counter in front of Dean.

"Oh God." Dean turned away. "Don't show me that this early in the morning."

Brent stepped behind Dean and turned him to face his reflection. "Morning has little to do with it. You look like this most of the time. Your face is always drawn, and the bags are taking up permanent residence under your eyes. Your clothes hang on you."

"But if I'm going to attract hot guys, I need to be able to fit into skinny jeans."

Brent groaned. "That isn't you. This whole thing with Dumbfuck needs to end. So he's getting married… big deal. You could be getting on with your life if you weren't determined to fuck it all away, literally. Instead of the bars, go somewhere else, meet someone, say hello, stop fucking around, and maybe you'll be the next one to get hitched." Brent leaned closer but jumped back away from Dean's toxic breath. "God, man." He waved his hand in front of his face.

Dean turned away from the mirror. "Would you stop lecturing me? I get that shit from everyone. My parents call me all the damn time to ask why the fuck I'm throwing my life away, and work is crap right now. I thought I'd get some sympathy and understanding from my friends." He set the mug on the counter and pushed back the stool. "Jesus!" Dean stood and stormed into the other room.

Brent groaned softly. He'd tried, but there was no use attempting to explain to Dean that it was because he was his friend that he had to say something. Dean wouldn't hear of it. Shit. Now Dean was mad at him. Not like that was anything new. Dean's temper had a hair trigger lately.

Brent finished getting ready, and Dean slumped out of the bedroom. He downed the last of his coffee and groaned. "You don't need to take your anger out on me," Brent told him as levelly as he could. "I was only trying to help." He waited for Dean to lift his gaze and then met it with one as steely as he possibly could.

"Thank God it's Saturday and I don't have to go to work," Dean growled.

"Are you okay to drive? You don't look very well." Brent wasn't going to let Dean take off and then have his friend joining Scott in the hospital. "I can take you home on my way out."

"I'm fine. Really." Dean smiled, though Brent knew it was forced, especially with the lack of energy in his eyes. Brent hated seeing his friend like this and wanted to help, but there was nothing he could do as long as Dean wasn't willing to help himself. "Don't worry. I'm fine. I slept well and drank lots of water. I really am okay." Dean's smile got brighter. "Thanks for looking out for me." He hugged him and Brent felt much better about him driving. Dean said goodbye before he left the apartment, and Brent got his stuff for work.

Once he was set, he drove to the hospital, went up to the desk, and explained that he was there to see Scott Spearman. He was given a wristband, then followed directions to the ICU. Brent told the nurse at the desk who he was there to see, and she took him back.

Scott was in a small room, the bed surrounded by monitors with a number of tubes and cords hooked to him. His usually robust cheeks were sallow, his normally intense eyes closed, his pouty lips pale.

"Please remain quiet."

"Of course," Brent said as he pulled forward the small chair and sat next to the bed. He didn't ask her a bunch of questions about how he was doing because Brent knew she couldn't really tell him anything without specific written permission.

The nurse checked Scott over and left the room.

"Hey, Scott. It's Brent. I wanted to stop by and see you." He blinked as Scott's chest slowly rose and fell. "I read somewhere that people can sometimes hear things when they're out like this. So I hope you get better." He turned to make sure no one was around to hear him, then leaned closer. "I should have told you how I felt." He sniffed and took one of the tissues from the box on the tray table. He reached for Scott's hand and slid their fingers together. Brent probably didn't have a right to do that, but he wanted Scott to know he was there.

To his surprise, Scott's fingers squeezed his just a little. At first, he wasn't sure it was real, but Scott did it again. Brent gently rubbed the back of his hand but received no further movement in response.

"Are you Brent?" a man who had to be Scott's dad asked. He looked so much like him, only an older, more weathered, and very worried version, with touches of gray in his hair.

"Yes," Brent whispered, setting Scott's hand back on the blankets, his cheeks heating. "I was just trying to make a connection with him. I think he might have squeezed my hand a little." He wondered what Scott's dad—and then his mom as she followed him inside—must be thinking with him holding Scott's hand.

"He did that last night before we left. It's the only indication that we've had that he's there and knows we're here." Scott's mother approached, and Brent stood to give her the chair. She sat, gently stroking Scott's hand. "Is there something between you and my son?" She lifted her gaze, and it was like she was looking deep into his soul. It was immediately evident where Scott got his amazing eyes, even if hers were red and definitely filled with concern. "I heard what you were saying to him before we came in."

"Don't mind Carolyn. She has bat-like hearing sometimes." Reggie stepped to the other side of the bed, looking at Scott. If Brent were to hazard a guess, Reggie was willing his son to wake up. The worry and sheer willpower were written on the lines of his furrowed brow.

"Reggie," she said gently, then turned to Brent. "Scott talked about you all the time. I think he may have a crush on you." She looked him over. "I can see why, but aren't you a little old for him?"

Brent nodded. "That's why nothing ever happened." He turned back to Scott, not believing he was having this conversation. "I'm his manager and…." There were so many reasons why he'd never said anything to Scott, though all of them seemed too stupid now. Scott lay on the bed, largely unmoving, and none of Brent's reasons mattered. All that did matter was that Scott would recover and get better again.

"I see," she said, as though there were some great meaning behind Brent's words. "He told me about the time the oil gun sprang a leak and he got sprayed. You got the oil shut off and him out of there and cleaned off so fast, before it could get in his eyes."

"He told you that?" Brent closed his eyes, stifling a groan, as his cheeks had to be turning beet red. He'd cleaned Scott off and had damn near kissed him just because he was relieved Scott was all right. Just as he'd gotten close, Scott had opened his eyes and their gazes had met, but Brent had backed away. His cowardice had taken over the way it usually did.

Carolyn nodded. "He said you were gentle and made sure he was okay before everything else. Then you apparently took apart the equipment, fixed it, and made sure that didn't happen again." She smiled. "Scott tells us stories about work all the time, and many of them featured you."

What was he supposed to say to that? Brent wanted to hide and lick his wounds somewhere. It seemed that the teasing and flirting Scott had done was more than just playing. Brent had never been sure, but now he knew. Scott had cared and might have been truly interested, but now it might be too late.

"That's so nice to know." Brent couldn't help looking at Scott and wondering what might have been if he had just had the guts.

CHAPTER 2

SCOTT FELT like hammered shit. Well, maybe that was an understatement. He drifted from pain to a euphoria of sorts but was scared to move. Each breath felt tight, and he was afraid to inhale more deeply. His ears rang with a high-pitched, annoying sound that thankfully seemed to be dissipating. Other than that, the world was quiet, which was a relief. He was so tired, he didn't want to open his eyes, but yet something deep inside told him he should.

A hand slipped into his. The grip was gentle but firm. He didn't think it was his mother's. It could have been his dad's, but he wasn't sure. The touch didn't last long, but it was enough for him to center his mind on it. Scott concentrated and tried to move his fingers, but it felt like they were disconnected. No, that wasn't it. Like there was a thick fog around his brain. He put all his thought power behind it, and the fog lifted, at least in that direction. He could feel the touch again, a slight squeeze, and he answered it—he knew he had. So he tried his other hand, making the connection there, moving his fingers. He took a deeper breath, concentrating on controlling his lungs. Then he worked on the fog elsewhere. He moved his feet. He knew it. The fog was retreating, and Scott needed to see where he was, so he cracked his eyes open.

The light was too much so he closed his eyes, groaning. The grip on his hand became more insistent. He cracked his eyes open again, and this time the light was dimmer. Deliberately, he opened them, focusing on the ceiling, and then slowly turned his head. The first face he saw was Brent's, and standing next to him was his mother. He looked down at his hand and saw Brent held it.

Was he dead? Scott closed his eyes, trying to figure out what was real. He had to be dead, because that was the only way Brent would be holding his hand. Scott smiled as twinges of pain washed over him. He couldn't be dead if he hurt, so that meant this was real.

He opened his eyes. Brent was still there, only now it was his mother holding his hand. Still, Brent smiled at him.

Scott attempted to speak, but his throat hurt and was so dry that nothing came out. His mother's lips moved, like she was trying to say something, but Scott heard nothing. He tried to speak again, but his mother gently stroked his shoulder, and Scott let his eyes close. He needed to check to see if there was still fog that he needed to get rid of. When he concentrated on the sounds around him, he heard nothing.

A chip of ice crossed his lips, and he sucked it into his mouth, letting the cold water coat his tongue and then slide down his throat.

"I can't hear," he finally said.

His mother turned to his father, and she might have gasped before putting her hand over her mouth. Scott turned to his dad, who put up one finger and then slowly stroked his arm. He didn't know what his dad said, but Scott followed his father with his eyes until his father stood at the end of the bed. He said one word, *doctor*, and Scott sighed. Then his dad left the room, and Scott turned back to his mom and Brent.

Scott closed his eyes as fatigue and pain washed over him. He waited for it to pass and cracked his eyes open once again. Someone came in and began asking questions. He saw her lips moving but heard nothing at all. His mother seemed to be answering.

Then a nurse, about his mother's age, leaned over in front of him. She held up a syringe.

"It hurts." His head, his chest, all over. At least he could talk. He hoped he was talking anyway. He could feel the vibrations of his own words, but that was all.

She held up one finger and then, after a few seconds, all ten.

"Hurts. A lot," Scott answered, closing his eyes yet again. As soon as he did, he was cut off from everything. He heard nothing and could see nothing. Then the pain began to recede. He opened his eyes and turned to his mother, who was chewing on her lower lip. She only did that when she was extremely nervous. Then he turned to Brent, who always told him the truth.

Brent leaned forward, touched his hand, and lightly stroked it.

"Is this for real?" Scott asked.

Brent smiled gently and nodded, gripping his hand a little tighter. "It's... okay," he said very slowly, and Scott was able to read his lips.

He nodded and groaned again as a wave of unadulterated fear swept over him. He couldn't hear... he was deaf. Tears filled his eyes and ran down his cheeks. Scott swallowed hard and let them fall. There was nothing he could do. His eyelids grew heavy and, unable to stay awake any longer, he dozed off just as his mother brushed his tearstained cheeks.

A STROKE down his arm sometime later woke him again. This time a doctor stood in front of him. He held up his notebook, with words printed on the page: *I'm Dr. Simpson. I want to run some tests. Just tell me if you can hear anything.*

"Okay," Scott said, looking around at the others and then closing his eyes. But he heard nothing other than the slight ringing. "I don't hear anything. There is a ringing, though, but it's growing softer." He continued listening, straining for any sound to reach him, but there was none at all.

Dr. Simpson touched his hand, and Scott opened his eyes. Then Dr. Simpson wrote and held up his notebook again. *I am going to run some tests. There is swelling in your brain. We relieved the pressure. We will see if the pressure has gone down. The hearing loss may be temporary. Just relax. I will help you any way I can.*

"Thank you." Scott didn't know what else to say.

Dr. Simpson wrote again. *Please take it easy. We need you to sleep, rest, and give your head a chance to heal. We relieved the pressure and are monitoring it.*

Scott read the note. "I understand."

You rest now.

"I'll do my best. But I'm scared."

Brent reached for Dr. Simpson, and he passed him the notepad. Brent wrote furiously and then turned around the page. *Of course you're scared. But you're alive, and we're all grateful for that. You have a lot of support and people who care for you.* Brent took his hand and squeezed, then turned the page away, flipped it over, and wrote some more. *You need to concentrate on getting better and not worrying about anything. You have a lot of healing to do, and we'll be there for you. All of us.*

"Okay," Scott agreed, getting tired.

Don't make me get James and Lee. After that Brent had drawn a smiley face. *There is still a lot no one knows, so be as patient as you can.*

Scott yawned. "I'll do my best, boss." He tried not to think of what would happen to him if he couldn't hear again. This was overwhelming, and as fatigue set in, he closed his eyes, trying not to cry like a child.

SCOTT WOKE some time later when he was wheeled out of the room and down for some sort of tests where they put him through large machines and wrote notes to tell him not to move. He just kept his eyes closed and pretended nothing was happening. That was easy.

By the time they brought him back to the room, Scott was tired again and went back to sleep. This time he dreamed, and he could hear. Brent was there, smiling at him, and they were at a beach together, happy. That was one of his fantasies. He and Brent would go away to a warm beach, and when there was no one around, they'd race into the water and Brent would spin him off his feet into his strong arms, where no one would hurt him again.

Scott snapped his eyes open, and he looked around, breathing deeply. His mom and dad were still there, but Brent was gone, and Scott missed him. His mother took his hand, and his dad held up a sign for him.

They are moving you to a regular room in a few minutes. He smiled, and Scott nodded.

"That means I'm doing better?" He listened to see if he could hear anything at all, but only the soft ringing was there.

His dad wrote some more. *Yes. The swelling is going down and they said your ribs are beginning to heal. You're going to be sore for a while.* He flipped the page and wrote again. *The doctor said he's hoping your hearing will come back once the swelling goes down more.* He shook the page, probably for emphasis, but if Scott could do everything else and still not hear, then that was likely bullshit.

He bit his lower lip and said nothing. His mom and dad seemed so hopeful, and he didn't want to crush them, even as he closed his eyes and wondered what the hell he was going to do.

"Where is Brent?" Scott asked, forcing his eyes open.

His dad scratched on the page. *He had to go to work, but he said he'd be back up to see you soon.*

"He's nice," Scott said.

His mother stroking his hand, pulling his attention to her. "Do you like him?" she asked, speaking slowly. It wasn't hard to read her lips since he was half expecting the question.

"Geez, Mom," he whined, not wanting to talk about stuff like that now. She continued looking at him with that mom gaze. "He's my boss and it wouldn't be right. At least I'm assuming that's what Brent would say." He pursed his lips. Scott had always hoped Brent would come around, but that wasn't going to happen now. Not fucking likely. His entire body tensed, and he winced at a shot of pain. Thankfully it retreated and his muscles relaxed as the pain subsided. "It doesn't matter now." He turned away and closed his eyes, effectively cutting himself off from them.

THE BED shook under him, and a man moved into his field of vision. Scott followed him with his eyes as he unhooked some of the tubes and things from the wall and placed them on the bed next to him. Then he was moving, and Scott lay there with his eyes closed and went along for the ride. It was too much effort for him to ask any questions, and they didn't matter anyway.

It didn't take long before he was in his new room. It was larger, with a sofa of sorts near the window, as well as a large chair next to his bed.

"Thank you," Scott told the nurse as she hooked everything back up. She was probably talking to his mom and dad, but it all went by him. He figured he was going to need to get used to that. She leaned into his line of sight and put up her fingers. "Six," Scott said, and then the pain slipped away and his eyes grew heavy once more.

SCOTT DIDN'T remember his dreams when he woke, but Brent was sitting on the sofa when he opened his eyes. No light came through the window, and other than the soft light near the sink area, the room was dark.

Brent took his hand as the haziness of sleep slipped away.

"Why are you here?" Scott asked. "I know you're my boss and all, so it's rude of me to ask you to leave. I've worked with you for two years and you knew I was interested, but you put me off." He turned to Brent, because it was his only way of getting any sort of reaction. "I flirted with you, and you turned the other way. Sometimes you flirted back, but that was all. I don't understand why I have your attention now." Was it some sort of pity thing?

Brent leaned forward on the sofa, slightly over the bed. He said something, and of course Scott had no idea at all what he wanted. Not that it mattered.

"Maybe you were right."

Brent shook his head, and for a second, Scott tried to figure out what the gesture meant, but he was still too tired and probably a little drug-hazed. This whole getting hurt thing really sucked.

Brent held up a notepad in front of him. *I was wrong.*

"That doesn't matter now. Right or wrong, things are what they are. I can't hear, and there isn't anything I can do about it." Scott turned away, tired and ready to be alone so he could wallow in some self-pity for a while. "S... so you should go back to your life and your friends, and leave me to try to figure out what the hell I'm going to do with mine, because it's pretty damn clear that everything has changed for me." He looked back at Brent. "I know what my dad said the doctors said, but I think that's bullshit. He's trying to keep my hopes alive and spare me the pain of the truth." Scott worried his fingers over his palms. Part of him hoped he was wrong.

"I don't know what will happen," Brent mouthed slowly, and at least Scott knew that was the truth.

"Will you tell me the truth?" Scott asked, and Brent nodded. "Everything is going to change for me. I know that. I can't expect you or anyone…." He took a deep breath, knowing he needed to get this out. "Whatever duty you feel you have… why you're spending hours here at the hospital instead of going out and living your life? It isn't real. Okay? There's nothing for you here anymore. We never gave what the… whatever it was that we felt all these months… a chance, so don't think you need to try now because you feel sorry for me."

Brent swallowed, and Scott watched as some of the light dimmed in Brent's eyes. But he didn't stand or make any effort to leave. Instead, he sat back on the sofa, crossing his arms over his chest.

Scott rolled his head until he was staring at the ceiling. He didn't want to watch television and had slept so much that, for now at least, he was wide-awake. Scott wasn't sure what Brent was doing, but that didn't matter. If he wanted to sit with him, fine. Scott had said his piece and had no illusions about where things stood between them. Brent was his boss, or had been his boss, since Scott had no idea how he was going to be able to do his job without being able to hear. The plain truth was, everything in his life had been upended in one fell swoop and he was going to have to learn to deal with all of it. The more he thought about it, the closer the tears got to the surface.

Then the pain medication kicked in again, and sent him to dreamland soon enough. At least there he could hear.

SCOTT LAY in bed, getting squirmy as Dr. Simpson and a nurse stood nearby. They looked him over and then the nurse began unhooking some of the tubes and things he was attached to. The best part was that the IV was being removed. He'd been up walking a little the day before, but now, apparently, he'd be allowed to get up to use the bathroom as long as he had help. They seemed pleased with how things were going. Scott took that as a big step forward in his healing and a step back in the hope that his hearing would return.

Dr. Simpson had still said he was hopeful it would return in time, but Scott found it harder and harder to believe. The ringing was still there, but gradually it had gotten softer, and Scott felt whatever hope he might have had was dissipating. He closed his eyes, gritting through the discomfort and pain. Then they were done, and Dr. Simpson gave him a smile and a thumbs-up.

You're doing very well, he wrote, and Scott nodded.

"Can I get up to use the bathroom now?" He had been so sick of having tubes and stuff attached to him, especially the catheter.

The nurse helped him out of bed and escorted him to the bathroom. She waited until he was situated, showed him the call button, and then closed the door.

Scott did his business like a normal person. God, he was grateful for this. His ribs were still sore, so he gingerly stood and flushed. Then he washed his hands before opening the bathroom door.

His mom and dad both turned to him and then stepped back to let him get to the bed. He sat carefully on the edge and got back in, breathing heavily from the exertion. He would have sworn he'd run a race.

Once he got settled and the nurse checked his dressing, his mother patted his arm and waved. Then she took his dad's hand, and they left the hospital room.

When Scott had exited the bathroom, he hadn't seen Trevor and James, but he couldn't miss them now.

Trevor approached the bed and bent down to hug him carefully. He didn't try to say anything, and there was nothing Scott needed from him other than some of his strength.

James came over and hugged him as well, then placed one of the fancy tablet-type laptops on his tray table, keeping the keyboard to the side and the display where Scott could see it.

Trevor made adjustments and then kissed James on the cheek before sitting down.

You and I are going to have a talk, James typed.

"Okay." Scott smiled. "Why do I feel like I'm being taken to the principal's office?"

Ha, ha…. No. I want to talk to you about what's going to happen, and I want to give you the chance to tell me how all of this is making you feel. James paused, and then more words appeared. *I was younger than you when I lost my sight, but I could see once. So I know what I'm missing, just like you. It's a loss that you need to grieve for.*

"You mean like someone died?"

Yes! Exactly. Your mom told me the doctors are still hopeful that your hearing might return, but you are going to have to prepare for the possibility that it might not. That means you will need to learn to navigate the world as a deaf person.

Scott closed his eyes as the tears started, and Trevor took his hand firmly in his. Scott turned to him but tilted his head toward the screen.

I know it's hard, and you're going to be angry and pissed off at the world. I was. That's normal. But always remember that your family and everyone who knows and loves you are here to try to help you. They care. James removed his hands from the keyboard and slowly made his way to the side of the bed. He leaned over and hugged Scott once again, this time with intensity. He didn't hold him tightly, just firmly, and he didn't back away.

The dam that had been building up inside him burst, and Scott put an arm around James as the tears flowed freely. Damn, he'd thought he'd been handling this so well, and all it took was James to be with him for five minutes and he was coming apart. He sniffed as James continued to hold him while more and more of the eggshell-thin dam came crashing down.

"What do I do?" he asked, and James released him gently and felt his way back to the computer.

You help others help you!

Scott sniffed once more as James continued typing.

I have some contacts at the School for the Deaf, and I've already messaged Grant, the head of the school. I will give his contact information to your mom and dad, and you can set up classes for all three of you to start sign language. They will also teach you to read lips.

"What if my hearing eventually comes back?"

Then you will have a skill that will serve you well for years to come. James paused, and Trevor moved closer to him. They had a quick conversation, and then James resumed. *You're luckier than most. You were able to hear and thus learned to talk. So that gives you an advantage over people who were born deaf.*

"But I want to hear," Scott said.

James turned to him and actually scowled. He didn't have a lot of facial expressions, so when he reacted that strongly, Scott was pretty sure he'd pissed him off.

Tough titty, James typed, and Scott's mouth hung open. *We get the lot in life that we're dealt. I didn't ask to become blind, but it happened, and now I help others. You need to pick yourself up and face what's ahead of you straight on. No mollycoddling or acting like a child. You're an adult. You can be mad at the world if you want, but pull on your big-boy panties and do what you have to do.*

"Jesus. Are you this way with your students?"

When I have to be. Life isn't going to be as easy now. The strong, smart, and resilient thrive despite any adversity put in their way. I know you're one of those people. Remember, I saw how you helped Lee.

Scott went cold. "Lee. Oh God. What am I going to do?" He groaned. "How am I going to talk to him? I can learn sign language, but he can't see it, and I don't know if he has a computer like you do. Besides, what good is that going to do us when we're working on cars?" He turned to Trevor. "How am I going to be able to work?"

Trevor crossed his arms and spoke briefly to James, who typed for him. *You'll work it out. Nothing is insurmountable if you want it and are willing to work at it hard enough. You can't hear and Lee can't see. Complement each other and work it out. He can hear you just like I can, and Lee does have one of these computers. I helped get it for him.*

Scott sighed, unconvinced. "Okay, if you think so."

Things aren't going to be easy. But if you care about your friendship with Lee, you'll work out a way. James paused, then started a new line. *Brent told me to tell you that he and Lee will come up tonight to see you.*

Brent had been there every day, and each time Scott wondered what he wanted. "That's nice." He smiled, genuinely happy. "Brent usually comes after work. I've told him it isn't necessary, and above the call of duty for my boss, but he comes anyway."

Trevor and James had a quick conversation and then James began typing again. *Brent was the person who asked us to come talk to you. He wants you to do well.* James considered his words, actually putting his finger to his lips before lowering his hand again. *We all do. The more friends and people who care for you to support you, the better off you are.* James seemed to be mulling something over. *I want to tell you a story. It may be a little awkward this way, but you need to hear it.*

"I do?" Scott felt strange, like he was talking to a computer, his attention riveted to the screen.

Yes. See, you know I went blind at twelve. Well, after that, my mom was there for me. She did everything that she could to help me. And I came to rely heavily on her.

"I can understand that."

James nodded and continued typing. *Two things happened. I wanted to be independent, and that hurt her because she thought*

I was turning my back on her. And then once she accepted that, she began to resent me because she'd spent all her efforts helping me. It was pretty weird. The thing is, I relied on my mother for just about everything and I think it might have burned her out.

"What are you trying to tell me?" Scott asked.

James hesitated, his hands on the keyboard. *Independence is one thing, but we'll always need help in one way or another. The world is designed for people who can both see and hear, so navigating it can be tough sometimes. The bigger our support group, the better. Don't write off anyone who is willing to stand by you and help you.* James held out his hand, and Trevor took it and gave it a squeeze before letting go. Then James went back to typing. *I didn't figure things out until I met Trevor.*

"I promise to do my best."

Good. What questions do you have?

"You don't happen to know how long it takes to learn sign language?" Scott asked.

James turned to Trevor, who spoke to him briefly. *He says about two years for beginner to intermediate level, at least the internet says so. It's a whole new language, and your entire family should learn. But if you attend the School for the Deaf, you'll probably pick it up faster because you'll be around people who use it all the time.*

Scott sighed and closed his eyes. This was so overwhelming.

James touched his hand. *You're a smart man—you'll figure out ways to communicate with people. You just need to be patient. Sign language isn't going to help you with anyone who doesn't understand it. Just give yourself a chance. It was the same for me when I needed to learn Braille.*

He skipped to the next line. *Anything else? We can always talk any time you want.*

"Thanks, James. I was really lost. That's probably normal too, I suppose."

It's only been a few days and it's a lot to digest. Give yourself a break and take things one day at a time. James closed the computer and came over to hug him again. Without a word, James managed to convey that everything truly was going to be all right. Hell, if James could manage to thrive, then Scott would do the same.

Feeling better and at least a little in control of something, along with the initial formulation of a plan, Scott decided that being proactive and contacting the people at the school might be good for him.

He said goodbye to Trevor and James as they got ready to leave. Trevor probably would have ruffled his hair if it wasn't for the bandages, but he leaned close, putting his cheek to Scott's. It was such an intimate and caring gesture that Scott felt the tears welling once again.

"James, give me a hug, please," Scott said, and James took Trevor's place, stroking his arm. He didn't need words to know how both of them felt about him, and it was pretty special. Trevor was his ultimate boss, but Scott knew he had his support. Then James backed away, and Scott followed them with his eyes as they left the room and his parents came back inside.

His mother fussed over him for a few minutes and then sat down in the chair, presumably once she knew he was okay.

"I think they helped, Mom."

She reached for a pad and pen. *You have some very nice friends. All of them.*

Scott smiled, his eyes heavy. "Thanks, Mom." He yawned and closed his eyes. His head ached a little, and he hoped some rest and some time without having to think would help. It didn't take long before he'd dozed off.

HE WASN'T sure how long he was out, but they were bringing dinner. Scott ate slowly, the food tasteless, so he only had enough to make the hunger in his belly go away. After that he pushed the tray aside and lay back, dozing once again. Being in a world of silence, once he closed his eyes, it was remarkably easy to fall to sleep. There was nothing to disturb him, and unless he was touched, he could exist in his own little world for a while.

A TAP on his shoulder pulled him out of his nap, and he woke to Lee's smile. Scott sat up and pulled his best friend into a hug. It startled Lee for a second, but then he hugged him back.

"They said you were coming, and I'm so glad to see you." Damn, he wanted to hear what Lee was saying, but he didn't need to. Lee's shoulders shook, and Scott looked over to Brent, who was looking down at him with a half smile and tears running down his cheeks. That told him a lot about how Lee was reacting. "I'm going to be okay. Everything works except my ears, though they don't seem to know why, other than the swelling in my brain must have affected that part." He didn't want to let Lee go. A lot of people thought they were more than friends, but neither he nor Lee thought of the other that way.

Brent wrote on a notepad and showed it to him. *He was so worried.*

"It's okay. I'm going to be okay. I promise that once I get out of here, we'll figure out how you can talk to me, and then we can start working together again. I'll be your eyes and you be my ears." Scott patted Lee on the shoulder, and Lee lifted his head, smiling at him and nodding.

Lee turned away, and Brent wrote and held up another page. *I've been keeping your tools and things just where you left them... where we left them.*

Scott continued hugging Lee because it was the best method of communication they had, and Lee still seemed upset. "Hopefully they'll let me out of here in a few days. They want to make sure that there isn't any infection in my head and that my ribs are healing well. When they do, you can come over. James said you have a tablet like his, so we can talk that way."

Lee nodded and stepped away to stand next to Brent. A nurse came in to check him over, and then Scott and Lee chatted for a while before Lee got ready to go. Lee and Brent said goodbye, hugging him again, and then left the room.

His mother picked up the pad from where Brent had put it, then set it down when she was done writing. *Like I said, you have really good friends. Especially Brent.*

Scott squinted. "He stood there and didn't come close at all. He never even talked to me."

She snatched up the paper and wrote again. *There are a lot of ways to show that someone means something to you.* She flipped the page and wrote some more. *It was Brent who arranged with us for your friends James and Trevor to come up here and talk to you. He also brought Lee so he could see you.* She fixed him with a stare and then set the notepad on the rolling table. She leaned over the bed to kiss him on the forehead. His mom looked like she'd aged a decade in the last few days, but some of the worry had gone out of her face and she looked less haunted.

"Good night, Mom." He took her hand. "Thank you for everything." He squeezed it and let her go. Then he turned to his dad and hugged him. "Thanks, Dad. I'm going to get through this. I don't know how yet." He handed his dad the paper James had given him. "He's a friend of James's at the School for the Deaf. James said he messaged him. So maybe he can help me."

His dad patted his hand and nodded. For a few seconds, Scott thought he saw pride in his father's eyes. Then he leaned down and hugged him. His dad had never been a tactile kind of man, but Scott was so glad that seemed to be changing.

His mom and dad left the room, and he was alone.

Scott reached for the pad his mother had been using and flipped through the messages until he found the one about Brent.

He stared at it, trying to make sense of why Brent would do this for him. His heart leaped with hope, but he pushed it away. He'd had a lot of hopes dashed in the last few days. Brent was being nice. Nothing more. At least he told himself that, but he didn't want to believe it. Hope kept springing up like a well inside him, not matter how much it hurt when those hopes were dashed time and time again.

CHAPTER 3

BRENT WANDERED the service bays of the station, making sure everything was as it should be and checking that none of the guys needed help. Lee was working with Clyde, one of the younger mechanics, and they got along fine together. Lee was liked by all of the guys who worked at the garage, and they all looked out for him. Clyde was patient, but the two of them didn't have the deep symbiotic chemistry that Lee and Scott had. Still, it was good to see Lee working. He always seemed happy here, but with Scott gone, so was some of the light that made Lee sparkle.

"Scott is coming home today," Lee said as Brent approached where he and Clyde were working on an old Dodge Dart. It was the owner's baby, and she'd had it since it was new and wasn't willing to part with it.

"Yes. I talked to his mother this morning, and she said she planned to bring him by here on his way home so he could see everyone." Damn, Brent was a hell of a lot more excited than he had a right to be. He was thrilled that Scott was coming home, but….

No, he was determined to push the doubts away. When Scott had been hurt, Brent had told himself that he was going to stand up for what he wanted. Every time he closed his eyes, it took him just a few seconds to pull up an image of the two of them, maybe together at one of the festivals at the Summerfest Grounds, Scott smiling. It didn't matter that Scott couldn't hear. That was just part of who he was now.

"Brent, are you all right?" Lee asked as he slowly righted himself from under the car's hood. "You've been standing there without moving. Is something wrong with the car? Am I doing something wrong?" He often asked that question, always afraid his lack of sight would get in the way.

Brent needed to remember that Lee might not be able to see, but he had some sort of radar sometimes. "No. I'm fine. And of course you haven't done anything wrong." He'd just been woolgathering when he needed to be working. Brent was doing that a lot lately—well, that and beating himself up for two years of sitting around on his cowardice. He lightly placed his hand on Lee's shoulder just to reassure him. Brent normally wasn't a touchy-feely guy at work, but Lee was the exception. He needed to be touched just so he could be connected with. It was something Brent had needed to learn and had come to understand. With Lee, touch was welcome.

Brent waited as the guys went back to work, and then moved on. When he was done, he returned to his office to review the day's schedule of appointments, as well as the one for the week. He reviewed all the reporting data that Trevor needed and was deep in his files when his door opened. He expected to see Trevor, but as soon as he caught the scent of violets rather than oil, he knew it wasn't his boss.

"Sweetheart. You're always working and I never see you." His mom set her purse on the chair as Brent stood and came around his desk to give her a hug and a kiss on the cheek.

"You look good, Mom. I really like your hair." Brent turned his head to take in the slight red tint. "It's perfect for you."

She beamed. "Thank you for noticing, dear. Your father never did." She hugged him again. "So, how are you? I see you aren't dead. You could call me once in a while."

"I talked to you last week, and you know the whole phone thing works both ways." He mock glared at her and motioned her to a chair, while he leaned on his desk. "Other than to give me grief, what brings you by?"

"I need my car looked at. It's making a squealing sound sometimes." She lowered herself into the chair with a sigh.

His mother was in her late fifties and usually quiet. She hadn't changed her hairstyle in years, but the sunny floral dress she was wearing had to be new.

"So what gives with the new look? You look amazing."

She bit her lower lip. "I've… well…. One of the gentlemen at work. He's in accounting, and his wife passed a few years ago of cancer." She picked up her purse and placed it on her lap as a kind of shield. "He asked me out this weekend, and…."

Brent grinned and blinked a few times. "Are you going to do it?"

"Yes," she breathed. "Your father was an amazing man, but he's been gone a long time…." She opened her purse and pulled out a tissue. "I always thought that part of my life was over. I mean, there's no one who can ever replace Allan, but…." Her eyes sparkled. "I think it's time I tried living again. Mike and I have been having lunch a few times a week at the office. We've become friends of a sort. I knew Josephine, his wife, from office functions, and…." She wrung her hands. "What do you think?" She sounded so nervous.

Brent gathered her into his arms, hugging her tightly. "I think it's an amazing idea. And I'm happy for you." When he released her, she wiped her eyes one more time.

"I thought…." She sniffed.

Brent sighed. He'd spent years trying to deal with what happened to his dad. Holding years of guilt hidden down inside against his mother. "I know what you thought, and maybe some time ago, I would have felt differently. But you deserve to be happy again." He peered out the windows to the shop floor just to make sure everything was all right.

"There's someone you like, isn't there?" Her smile was genuine. "Has it been going on for a while?"

"Yes and no." Brent waited for her to sit down and then brought the wheeled desk chair around so he could sit by her.

He looked through the window at Clyde as he and Lee finished working on the Dart, and motioned him inside.

"Yeah, Brent?"

"Could you and Lee check out my mother's car? She says it's whining." He took the keys from her and handed them to Clyde.

"Sure thing." Clyde smiled, jingling the keys as he left the office.

"What is it you want to tell me?" his mother asked. "Your answer was enigmatic, and don't think you can change the subject." She dabbed her eyes and then put the tissue in the trash at the base of his desk.

"Well, you see… it's like this. Scott works here as a mechanic. He and Lee usually work together."

She turned, following Brent's gaze. "The one in the sunglasses? Isn't it dark for those?"

"Lee's blind. He and Scott work really well together. Lee lost his sight a few years ago. He was just about to get his license when he was blinded. Lee doesn't talk about it much. But you know James…." He waited for her nod. "Lee was one of his students, and Lee loved cars and can diagnose problems by sound faster than anyone. He and Scott are best friends."

His mother sighed. "Are you working up to something?"

"Yes." He sighed, and the words came tumbling out. "Scott is adorable, and he's so patient with Lee. He's cute and smart and funny. He picks on me, and I pick back. We flirt sometimes… but I know it isn't a good thing for me to be involved with anyone from work, so I stayed away."

"And he found someone else?" his mom supplied.

"No. I think Scott likes me, and I like him. He's special. He doesn't see me as just the boss, but as a person. You know? He always has. Last year when I was so sick, he called just to make sure I was okay." Scott wanted to try to make his mother understand. "He's a really great person and I really like him."

"Then what's the problem? Does your boss not approve?" She fidgeted a little, probably because he was making this like pulling teeth.

"Trevor says that as long as I don't let it interfere with work, it's fine. In fact, he told me to shit or get off the pot because of the tension and energy between us." Brent smiled. "But the thing is, Scott was rear-ended and hit his head and now he can't hear. He's coming home today."

His mother sighed softly. "You need to tell me what the problem is. Do you not want to be with him because he's deaf now?" She peered down her nose at him.

"Of course not. I've already looked into sign language classes so I'll be able to talk to him. They have them at the School for the Deaf, and I want to go. It takes two years minimum, but I'm a good student and I can learn." He sat on the edge of his seat, becoming more excited as he thought about broadening his horizons.

His mother cleared her throat. "Let me get this straight. You like Scott and you want to help him. Heck, you think enough of him as a person and an employee to go to take sign language classes for two years just so you can communicate with him. You've worked together for two years, scorching the wallpaper off the walls, and you never did anything about it." Her gaze grew sad. "Why?"

Brent bit his lower lip. "You know shit like that doesn't work out for me."

She narrowed her gaze at his language but didn't say anything, and for that Brent was grateful. "You have to do better than that."

Brent got to his feet and paced the small floor area. "You want me to say it? I was a coward, Mom. I hid behind the fact that I worked with Scott and used that as an excuse to do nothing about it at all." He stopped pacing and threw his hands in the air.

She stood and took his hands. "I thought we had worked through what happened with your dad. But I guess we've both been feeling the lingering effects for all these years." She squeezed his hands and stared straight into his eyes. "Now you listen to your mother. What happened is over and we have to move on... both of us. I'm going out with Mike, and I'm going to go on other dates. It's been fifteen years and I loved your father more than life itself. He's a hard man to get over, but we have to. You and I can't live our lives buried in the past. It's time for both of us to live again."

"I know, Mom. But I keep wondering if I'm good enough. If...."

She shook her head. "Coulda... woulda... shoulda. Bullshit!" She never swore, so this was something she felt really strongly about. "Live your life the way you want to now. None of us gets a chance to do things over again. If this young man can make you happy, then I want to meet him sometime." She smiled. "Listen to me. Second chances in this life are rare as hen's teeth. So if you get one with Scott, then you take it and see what happens. Your father would want that, and so do I." She squeezed his hands again. "I mean it."

Brent nodded, because arguing with her wasn't going to get him anywhere at all. But damn, he wanted some of her strength and fortitude. Wherever she'd gotten it, he wanted what she was having. "I'll do my best."

A knock on the office door interrupted their conversation. Brent opened it, and Clyde handed him his mother's set of keys.

"Some of the belts are getting a little old. We roughed them up a little and they stopped slipping. She should probably make an appointment to get them repaired, but it will be fine for a while."

"Thank you." Brent handed the keys to his mother.

"Set me up with an appointment and have the car looked over good. I have to go to Chicago and then St. Louis in a few weeks, and I want my car to be able to make the trip." She put the keys in her purse, pulled out two twenties, and handed them to Clyde. "Thank you, young man, for your help. Give one to Lee and tell him thank you as well." She smiled. Brent wanted to chastise her for tipping, but her expression said she was serious and it was best not to cross her.

"Thanks," Clyde said, then turned to him, confused. Brett shrugged, and Clyde smiled. "Oh, before I forget. Lee just got a message that Scott will be here soon. Is it okay if we take our break then so we can talk to him?"

"Not necessary," Brent said. "You take your break when you need to. We're all going to see Scott and wish him well." He smiled and Clyde grinned.

"I'll tell Lee."

"Awesome. And let everyone know. We want to show Scott that he's still a member of our family and that we miss him." Brent closed the door as soon as Clyde left, and his mother gathered her things.

"You take care of Scott, and if there's anything I can do, you be sure to let me know." She paused. "I think I'll bake some pies. His family is going to be very busy, and something homemade is just the ticket. I'll send it in with you, and you can make sure Scott gets it." She waved and left before Brent could argue with her.

His mother had turned from quiet and efficient to a whirlwind powerhouse. Brent knew he needed to meet Mike and thank him for whatever he'd done. She was a changed woman, and it was awesome to see. He really did like that she was standing up for herself and getting out there. Now he only had to figure out how he was going to make that happen for himself.

Excitement ramped up outside, and Brent figured Scott was here. He left his office as Lee, on Clyde's arm, hurried out to the car. Brent's breath hitched as Scott carefully got out, and then Lee was in his arms. Scott couldn't hear him, but that didn't stop Lee from telling Scott how much he missed him and that he was working with Clyde and they were doing well, but that he couldn't wait for his best friend to come back so they could spend time together. Scott simply held him and talked to Lee. It should have been one-sided, but Scott seemed to understand the emotion behind everything Lee was telling him.

Clyde, it seemed, had made some signs, and he hurried into the garage, pulled them out, and handed one to each person.

There were "We miss you, Scott!" "Get well soon." "Your service bay is waiting for you!" among others.

Brent knew the minute Scott saw them. He stopped, gasped, and then closed his eyes. The others all crowded around, patting his back, taking his hand. Some of the guys were usually standoffish, like Darryl. Straight but not narrow Darryl, who treated everyone with quiet respect but was never very demonstrative, hugged Scott, and dammit if Brent didn't possibly see a tear from him.

Brent strode over and stopped a little way from Scott. The others parted and let him through. He approached slowly, turning to peer inside the car. Scott's mother waited behind the wheel, so he walked to her and opened the door. "I have some coffee if you'd like some."

"That would be nice, but Scott and I can't stay long. He is supposed to take it easy." She slid out of the car to stand next to him.

"All right. They're all happy to see him in one piece." Brent was too, and even though Scott was still pale and walking stiffly, he was up and out of bed, and that was good. "We've all missed him."

She smiled and patted him on the shoulder. "I understand, and I'm happy to see that Scotty has so many friends."

"All right, everyone, Scott is just coming home from the hospital and we can't wear him out. I'm sure he'll be back soon."

They all gave Scott their well wishes as best they could and filtered away.

Brent reached into his pocket and pulled out a notepad. *They truly have missed you.*

"I see."

Brent hesitated and then wrote another note. He ripped it off the spiral and handed it to Scott as his mother guided him by the arm toward the car. Scott got inside, still holding his note, and Brent stood in the drive while they got in. He waved goodbye and stayed still until they'd pulled out of the drive. Then he went back into his office and closed the door. Brent needed to be alone, and he didn't want the others to see him nearly throw up over what he'd put in that note. He'd found some courage, and now he had to see if it would pay off or not.

AT THE end of the day, Brent closed the garage, going through his routine. He headed home, exhausted and yet nervous and keyed up. He'd finally had the guts to say something to Scott, at least in a way. It would have been nice if he would have been able to say the words to Scott in person. But then, he was coming to understand the fleetingness of what was said and the permanency of writing something down. That still didn't make him any less nervous.

At his apartment he cleaned up, did the dishes, dusted, vacuumed—anything to keep him busy. Brent checked his phone when he was done and found he'd missed a message.

Did you really mean it? Scott had sent.

Of course I did. Since this was one easy way to communicate with Scott, Brent imagined he was here with him and typed. *I've missed you every single day. When I sat at the hospital with you and you were asleep, I missed seeing your smile and hearing the way you used to tease and flirt with me.* He pressed Send and then waited. The screen showed that Scott was typing, but no message came through for a long time.

I don't know what to tell you. I liked you for a long time. But I knew you were my boss and thought you weren't really interested, and then Lee needed me and…. The message ended, but before Brent could figure out what to say, Scott began typing again. *I think you stayed away from me because you thought I was too young for you.*

Brent had stayed away because he was a damned coward and didn't have the guts to tell Scott how he felt. But his pride, what little he had, wouldn't let him say that.

I'm flattered that you care for me, Scott continued, *but everything has changed now, and I think you know that. It isn't fair for me to expect you or anyone else to get involved with me right now.*

As soon as those words hit Brent's screen, his stomach fell to the floor. He should have expected this kind of rejection.

When we flirted and worked together, I was a whole person. I could hear and we could laugh together. Now we can't do any of those things. I'm deaf, and I have to learn to live with that. There's a lot of rehab ahead of me, which is going to take a lot of my time. But I'm going to do it.

Brent swallowed hard, trying to think about what he wanted to say. *I know things have changed for you. They have for me too. But one thing James told me was that you can't do it on your own.* He set his phone on the table, walking to the kitchen and back just to try to clear his head. He snatched up the phone and began typing again. *I want to be there for you. As your friend, if that's all it can be.* His heart ached, but if that was all Scott felt he could give, then Brent would have to be satisfied with that. *But I will support you and do my best to try to help you.* He paused and then added, *If you'll let me.*

There wasn't a response for a while, and he wondered if maybe he'd pushed too hard or if Scott had decided to cut him off.

I think I'd like that. Everyone tells me that I'm going to need support.... After a brief moment, a new message started. *It's hard for me to ask for help sometimes.*

Not help. Support. There's a difference, Brent returned.

I guess so. It all sounds like help and me not being able to do what I used to do.

Brent closed his eyes and could almost see Scott sitting in a chair, his lips parted in consideration, eyes filled with worry as he typed. *You can do anything you set your mind to. Without a doubt. I've seen you open your world to Lee, and the two of you work as a team. That took intelligence and patience.* Brent doubted his attempts to build Scott up were working, at least for the moment. He suspected Scott was pretty worn out, and no one could blame him if he was depressed about his situation. Waking up and finding out you suddenly can't hear had to pull the rug out from under anyone.

I wish I could have this conversation in person, Scott sent, and the sadness came through. *I sit all day in silence. When I go outside, I can feel the wind but not hear it. There are no birds, just unending silence. And it's driving me crazy.*

Brent wanted to hold him and try to take away the longing that came through in Scott's words. *I can't imagine how you feel, so I'm not going to tell you that I do. I don't. Any more than I can understand fully how Lee feels.*

I know. I used to think how lucky I was that I could see. And I was proud to be his friend and work with him. There was a pause before another message came through. *I used to tell myself how lucky I was because I wasn't blind. And now I feel like complete shit.*

Why? Brent asked.

Because I used to think I was lucky. That Lee was someone I needed to look out for and help take care of. And now I'm the one that everyone is going to have to help. Sure, I can do most things. But I'll never hear anyone again—no music, no birds, no nothing. Brent was sure Scott was crying. *I will continue to help and watch out for Lee, and now he can do the same for me.*

Sometimes Scott surprised him so much. He was only in his early twenties, but he was mature and able to look at himself in a way that many others weren't. It only made Brent care for him more.

Suddenly an image of his dad flashed in his mind. He had been a sheriff's deputy, and Brent had worshipped him. Brent was fourteen when he'd figured out he was gay. Though they never talked about it, probably because Brent didn't have the words, he remembered his dad coming to his room one evening. Brent had been in bed and the room was pretty dark. His dad sat on the edge of his bed, something on his mind.

"Sometimes you have to accept shit you don't like because you can't do anything about it. Being an adult means you don't whine about it, but either turn it into an advantage or learn to live with it."

He remembered his dad's words clearly and sent them to Scott.

So now you're the one offering sage advice, Scott's message said, and Brent smiled.

It isn't mine. It's what I was told by my dad once, a long time ago. He didn't offer any more and hoped Scott didn't press. *How long before they think you can come back to work?* Brent missed seeing him every day.

They said it's going to be a few weeks. They want my ribs to heal, and the doctors want to see me every week for a while. They keep hoping that some of my hearing will come back, so they keep running tests to see what's going on. I hate it. Makes me feel like a lab rat. At least I'm cuter.

That hint of flirtation made Brent smile.

I should probably let you rest. But I'll try to see you soon. My mom said she was baking you a pie. Brent smiled as he sent that message, knowing how Scott felt about food.

Pecan?

Of course. It was his mother's specialty, and he'd brought some in for the guys on a few occasions.

Best news I've had all day... well, almost the best. Thanks, Brent. The display registered that another message was coming. *Mom told me I need to get some rest and she is going to split a gut if I don't listen to her.*

I'll talk to you soon. Brent waited and got a happy face in return.

Brent made himself some dinner, then watched television until his doorbell sounded. Brent checked the camera and buzzed Dean in, opened the door, waited, and pulled him into a hug.

"I thought you were mad at me, so I brought a peace offering." Dean held up a container of ice cream in a plastic bag. "And no drinking."

"Come on in." Brent took the bag, brought it to the kitchen, and slid it into the freezer until they were ready for it. "So what gives?"

"Other than you lecturing me?" Dean asked with a smart-alecky grin.

"Shit. You never listened before. Why now?" Brent grabbed a couple sodas and carried them over to flop on the couch next to Dean.

Dean took the soda and popped open the top. "After we talked and I felt like shit the following morning, I got to thinking. Of course, that didn't last very long, but I went out that night and was cruising this guy and realized I'd seen him before... at least eight times. And then I looked around and realized I knew most of the people there. We were all cruising each other in the same small group, and it's so incestuous. I turned around and left." Dean set his can on the table and turned sideways. "I'm just...."

Brent patted Dean on the shoulder. "Unlike the literary one, Peter Pan just grew up, and it's okay. You were happy for a while with Dumbfuck, and you'll be happy again. Only this time you'll be more careful about who you let into your heart."

"But what am I going to do with all this free time?" Dean asked with a wry grin.

"I don't know. You could take up knitting and make me some socks if you like. Or God forbid you could read and try to improve that useless thing two feet above your ass." Brent bumped Dean's shoulder.

"Actually, I thought I'd maybe try writing something. I was good at that sort of thing in college, and I spend my days writing code that's logical and all that. So I want to do something else."

"I know you can do whatever you want. What sort of things do you want to write?" Brent asked, curious.

Dean shrugged. "What I know best. What else? Stories about guys trying to find other guys." He smiled. "I saw some books at Outwords Books, and I think I'm going to try to write one of those. It probably won't be any good, but I think it will be fun." He beamed, and damn it all, it was the first time in a while that Brent had seen Dean truly excited over something.

"Hey, you have a great imagination, so do it and see what happens." Brent realized he'd been giving that advice to a lot of people lately.

"I know that." Dean grinned. "Speaking of putting your mind to something. What about your friend from work?"

Brent sighed softly. "I told him that I cared for him and that I was a fool to have waited. And I think we've decided to be friends."

"But that isn't what you want."

Brent nodded. "It doesn't matter what I want. His life is in complete upheaval at the moment. He's just found out that he can no longer hear. They keep hoping the condition will reverse, but I think he's giving up. Pressuring him into any kind of relationship isn't a good idea, so I'll be his friend and try to be there for him." Brent reached for a tissue and blew his nose, hoping to cover the well of emotion that rose inside him.

"You were always a good friend." Dean finished his soda, and Brent got up to get the ice cream. "Is this kid really worth all this angst and drama?" Dean called from the living room.

"Was Dumbfuck worth two years of slutdom?" Brent just had to ask.

Dean chuckled. "I get your point."

"The heart wants what the heart wants, and Scott is an amazing man who's going through hell at the moment. Would a real friend turn their back on him?" Brent got out two bowls and scooped ice cream for both of them. His phone beeped as he carried the bowls in, and Brent handed Dean his before peeking at the message.

"Your mom?" Dean asked.

"How did you know?"

"You have that freshly scolded look." He grinned, and Brent rolled his eyes dramatically. He had gotten his mother a new phone a year ago, and she liked to send text messages. Apparently it was now all the rage with her friends.

"She made a pie for Scott and says she wants me to take it over to him tomorrow." Brent sent his reply, promising he'd do that just after work, and she messaged back that she'd have it ready for him.

"Why does she have this pie thing?" Dean asked between bites of rocky road.

"You're complaining?" Brent teased, patting Dean's belly. "Let's find something to watch."

THE FOLLOWING afternoon Brent left the garage, having arranged for Darryl to close up, and headed to his mother's. If anyone had asked and demanded a truthful answer, he'd say he was nervous. When he arrived and went inside, she called out from her room and joined him in the kitchen in what looked like another new summer dress. Apparently, she was going all out for her new look.

"Mom, you look beautiful." He smiled and kissed her cheek. He liked the way his mother looked and that she seemed happy.

"I bought a few others as well." She turned slightly, gliding as she moved. "Do you need something to eat?"

"No, Mom, I'm fine." He watched her closely. "Besides, you look like you're getting ready to go out." He wasn't going to cramp his mother's style, as it were.

"Just meeting some friends for dinner." She had that glint in her eye, and Brent crossed his arms over his chest. "Okay. Mike invited me to a retirement dinner for one of the men who works for him. But I can stay here with you."

"Nope. It would be a shame to waste that dress and your newfound hotness on just me."

His mother blushed and it was adorable. "Go on and take the pie, then. I put it in a box, but be careful." She pointed to where she'd put it on the counter, and Brent lifted it before getting ready to leave.

"And I want a full report." He tried to scowl and failed.

His mother, however, succeeded. "I will do no such thing. Now go. After the hospital, he's going to want some real food, and the entire family will need to know they have friends who can help."

"His mother is cooking for him."

"Yes, and she's probably worrying herself sick. I know I would be." She patted his arm and paused, capturing his full attention. "Strength runs in our family. Your father had it, and this is testing yours." She released his arm and patted his cheek. "I know you'll make me proud." She picked up her purse and left with Brent, backing out of the drive right after he did.

Brent had looked up Scott's address and had already programmed it into his portable GPS. It didn't take long before he pulled up in front of a small ranch house in a beautifully landscaped lot in Glendale. He parked and got out. Brent had messaged Scott that he was coming, so it wasn't like he wasn't expected. Hell, Brent felt like a seventeen-year-old on prom night approaching the front door of his date's house. All that was missing was the tuxedo shirt digging into his neck and the shoes pinching his feet.

The door opened as he approached, and Carolyn held open the door. "He's been talking about this pie since you messaged him."

"It's his favorite, as far as I know." He stepped inside and handed her the box.

She took the pie out and inhaled as if it were a bouquet. She sighed. "That's wonderful."

"My uncle lives in Alabama and he has pecan trees. He picks the nuts, shells them, and sends them to my mother. So what she gets are extra fresh and better than anything from the stores." Brent looked around, wondering where Scott was.

Carolyn set the pie on the table and got out plates and glasses. "Please stay with us. Scott was tired and went to lie down. I need to wake him up." She shook her head. "I never realized just how many audible cues we have in our lives until I tried to put myself in Scott's shoes. He can't hear alarms. I ordered one that flashes, but he sleeps through the worst thunderstorms with all the lightning, so I don't know if that's going to do any good." She fussed but seemed more together than she had in the hospital.

"Is he doing well otherwise?"

"Healingwise, he's doing great. But I'm worried. He's already talking about sign language classes and looking into tools for the deaf. It's like he's given up hearing again, and I can't bear that. I want him to fight." She pulled out one of the kitchen chairs and collapsed into it.

Brent sat down as well and kept his voice light and soothing. "Fight against what? It isn't like he has an opponent or a bad guy. He can't will his hearing to come back or his nerves to heal. All he can do is deal with it."

"I share your concern, I really do," Reggie, Scott's dad, said as he came in, gently putting his hands on her shoulders. "But he wants to try to move on. I think that shows real maturity."

Brent directed his advice to Carolyn. "I think perhaps it isn't an 'or,' but maybe him doing both." She was an amazing person with so much strength and guts.

She didn't seem so convinced, and it wasn't Brent's place, as a guest in her home, to argue with her. "I'm just scared and I wish this had never happened. Excuse me," she said quietly and left the room.

"She's having a hard time with this. In some ways it's more difficult for her than Scott. He's her only child, and it hurts her to see him struggling and in pain. If it were something she could do anything about, she'd be fighting by his side like a tiger. But this…." Reggie pulled out the chair at the end of the table. "I know there's nothing else to do but move forward, but it's hard not to look back and wish things were different."

Brent kept quiet. If they needed to talk to someone, a near stranger, about what they were going through, that was fine with him. Brent would listen, but he was running out of advice that didn't sound like some worn-out cliché. Scott's parents needed to come to grips with what had happened as much as Scott did.

Brent was starting to think that maybe he should have become a therapist.

After taking the job with Trevor, Brent had learned that running a business was part manager and part therapist. His employees had problems that sometimes made it into work. He listened and gave them an outlet in the hope that whatever those problems were, they wouldn't interfere with their work. And it wasn't like he could turn off those skills. They had come as a surprise to him. Brent hadn't thought that was something he'd be good at, but he seemed to be, if the overall harmony in the garage was a judge.

"I wish there were magic words that would make things better."

"Me too." Reggie nodded, picking up a fork and nervously twirling it with his fingers.

Scott came in, moving slowly, followed by Carolyn, and Brent stood. Scott looked from his mom and dad to Brent. He seemed tentative and a little confused. Brent stepped forward, and Scott did the same, so Brent hugged him gently. Scott shook in his arms, but Brent didn't release him, letting Scott have some of his strength if that was what he needed. Neither said anything until Scott stepped away.

"Thank you for bringing the pie." He spoke more loudly than was necessary, but Brent ignored it. Carolyn made a lowering motion with her hand and moved toward the table. "Please tell your mom that I really appreciate it," he said more softly, almost too softly. Brent hoped Carolyn didn't motion again. He didn't care if Scott spoke a little loudly. He didn't want him to be self-conscious every time he said something.

Brent pulled a small notebook out of his pocket and wrote. *My mom told me to tell you that she has more pecans and can make you as many pies as you want. She loves baking and adores people who appreciate what she makes.* When Scott sat next to him, Brent slid the pad closer.

Carolyn cut the pie and served it with ice cream. Scott ate silently, with a smile on his face that said more than words could express.

"This is really wonderful," Carolyn said after taking a bite.

"I'll be sure to tell my mom." Brent smiled, a little uncomfortable under Reggie's and Carolyn's gazes. They seemed to want something, but he couldn't figure out what it was.

Instead, he wrote to Scott. *How's the healing going?*

Scott nodded. "I need to rest and let my ribs heal. I have an appointment in a few weeks with Grant at the School for the Deaf, and we're going to go over some possibilities. I think Mom and Dad are going to take sign language classes with me."

I am too. I called them as well, he wrote and turned to Scott so he could see his smile. *I know it will take time, but I want to be able to talk to you directly.*

Scott set down his fork with a loud clang on the plate. "You're going to go through all that for me?"

Brent barely heard him, and he wondered if Scott meant to voice the thought out loud. "Of course," he mouthed slowly, then smiled and shrugged.

Scott turned his attention back to his plate and picked up the fork. He finished off his pie and ice cream in silence while Scott's parents talked quietly between them about normal things. Once he had finished, Scott stood slowly and motioned for Brent to come with him. Brent excused himself and followed Scott into the neutrally decorated living room. He had to think of the last time he'd seen so many shades of beige in one room. Scott motioned to the sofa, and they sat down.

"You're really going to take those classes with me?" he asked quietly.

Brent nodded, taking one of Scott's hands and squeezing it to show him he was truly serious. He didn't want to write notes but rather wanted a connection with Scott. He needed him to understand he was serious. He'd do what was necessary to be a part of Scott's changing world. "It's important to me," he said slowly, and Scott nodded, leaning closer to rest his head on Brent's shoulder.

"Mom and Dad are doing their best for me, but they're doing what James said his mom did. They want to shelter me and take care of me."

Brent reached for the pad and held it where they could both see it. *You need to feel like the man you were before this happened instead of a child.*

Scott lifted his head, smiled, and nodded. "I'm not a child, and I hate that this happened. It's total shit." His voice got louder, and Carolyn stuck her head in the room for a second and then left. "I want to hit someone. Hell, I want to hit God, make him deaf to see how he likes it." Scott jumped to his feet. "I want to scream and yell, but I can't fucking hear myself. Everything is silent, expect for the buzzing that happens sometimes. The doctors say that's good because something is working, but I don't know. I think it's my head being angry with me." He rampaged, his hands trembling in front of him. He looked upward, shaking his fists as he seemed to fill with anger.

Carolyn came in again and hurried toward him, but Brent spoke up before she could get to him.

"Please let him work through this. He needs to let the anger out."

"But he could hurt himself. He isn't healed," she said forcefully.

Brent turned back to Scott, who stared at his mother, still seething, face red, anger rolling off him. "This is healing for me."

"Carolyn," Reggie called, his voice gentle and understanding. This was hard on everyone. "Come back in here and leave them alone."

She left the room reluctantly, and Scott shook from head to toe.

"What did I do to deserve this? Maybe God hates fags like the people at church think." He glared at the doorway. "I'm not going there anymore!" It was loud enough that Scott's folks were sure to hear it, which had to be Scott's intent. "Mom and Dad are cool with the whole gay thing, but the Sunday morning bigots aren't."

Okay, it was clearly Scott's time to vent, which was probably a good thing. Brent had found that most people expected those with a disability to be mild-mannered and quiet. Lee was quiet some of the time, but he had a temper. So did James, and clearly

Scott did as well. That was good, as far as Brent was concerned. It would serve him well.

Brent wrote quickly and handed Scott the paper. *You know God isn't like that. Accidents and diseases aren't handed out as punishment. They just happen.*

Scott threw it to the floor and stomped on it. "Son of a bitch, they could fucking happen to someone else!" He stopped and held his ribs. Brent hurried to him and helped him to the sofa. "I'm okay. Just some soreness." Scott leaned back, breathing heavily as tears leaked from the corners of his eyes.

Brent could only try to imagine how Scott felt. He had to let him work through this and get it out. There was little Brent could do, and that was the hard part for him, as well as for Scott's parents, who had to be sitting in the other room, listening intently to everything, probably worrying themselves half to death.

Brent retrieved the squashed notebook and picked up the pen he'd been using. *It's okay to get angry.*

Scott turned toward the kitchen and then back to Brent. He grabbed the pen, his handwriting barely legible as he scrawled his message. *Not really. Mom gets all "calm down, calm down" every time I feel anything. I'm angry and I don't want to be deaf, but I'm supposed to be quiet, sit still, and let them worry about it and figure out what I'm going to do. I'm supposed to get well, and they're supposed to figure shit out for me.*

Brent took the pen off him and wrote. *Bullshit! It's your life, and the decisions are yours. Make them, if that's what you want to do. You stood up for yourself and Lee three weeks ago. You've never had any problem with that. Why should you being deaf change that?* Scott's spunk was one of the qualities he admired. Brent pushed the notepad into Scott's hand, shaking it for emphasis, then pulled it back. *You don't need to be a dick about it, but knowing what you want is good. Tell them, tell me, tell anyone, and we'll help.*

Scott blinked at him. "You really think I can do that?"

Brent nodded. *I have faith in you, and you're the same person you were before the accident. In your heart you know that. So be that person!* He handed Scott the page and nodded.

Scott leaned back, closing his eyes. Brent was getting the idea that was part of his defenses. If Scott closed his eyes, he was shutting off everyone and everything. He couldn't hear and now he couldn't see, so he didn't have to deal with things… at least in that moment.

Brent waited for Scott to open his eyes and reengage with him. *Did you ever find out anything about the guy who hit you?*

Anger flared in Scott's eyes all over again, and he gestured as he talked, sitting forward. "He hit me really hard. The guy had to be drunk. I don't remember anything about that at all. Mom and Dad told me that there were pieces of the car that hit me at the scene. Other people called for help. Apparently they know the make and model of the car, as well as the color, from the parts left at the scene, but nothing else. No one actually saw the accident, I guess, or they didn't get the license plate."

Has anyone talked to you? Brent wrote.

"The police came to the hospital and asked me a bunch of questions, but they don't know anything. They're pissing in the dark and hoping they hit something." Scott growled. "I just want all this to be over and my life to go back to the way it was, but that isn't going to happen. I know that." He smacked the sofa cushion. "Some asshole gets drunk, drives, and hurts someone else. He just drives away and nothing happens. What the fuck is fair about that?"

Brent could have told him that little in life was fair. Him losing his dad at fourteen certainly wasn't fair. Yeah, he had the mom to end all moms. And she stepped up and tried to be both mom and dad to him. She learned baseball to help him with his throws and even helped coach one season when no one else would do it. When he was in ninth grade, they had a father/son thing at school and his mom showed up. At first he'd been mortified, but all the kids seemed to take it in stride, especially when another kid brought one of his mothers, because he had two. Brent's mom had stepped up as much as she could, but nothing was going to make up for the fact that his dad was gone, just like nothing was going to make up for what the idiot who had hit Scott and changed his life forever had done.

I wish I had an answer for you, he wrote. *I hope they catch him and hang him by his balls.*

"What if it was a woman?" Scott asked.

Then they can hang her by something else, as long as they make her pay. And I mean pay for a very long time. This was a lot for anyone to have to go through, and dammit, someone else was responsible.

Scott seemed drained, leaning back. "All I want is for whoever did this to know what they did and have to look me in the eyes. They need to be able to see and understand what their stupidity and callousness brought onto someone else. Oh, and I'd really like to kick them in the nuts!"

Brent couldn't argue with him. *What kind of car was it?*

Scott got up and went to the kitchen and returned with a piece of paper. "A red Chevy Malibu, about 2005 or 2006. At least that's what they think, but it could be any GM car from that period. I can't believe that no one saw it or could help. There are cars that go by there all the time. But apparently by the time people stopped to help me, the car was already gone."

Brent slid closer, wanting to comfort but not knowing how. This was pain right there, raw and livid, and what Scott needed was time to heal and deal with it. Which completely sucked, because he shouldn't have to go through this crap in the first place. Brent figured all he could do was be there and support him. *Give yourself a break and try to relax a little.*

"Now you sound like my mother," Scott retorted. At least he said it with a smile. Scott leaned forward to hug him, and heat shot through Brent like a bullet. Since Scott had been hurt, Brent had been hugging him to give comfort, but this was the first time Scott had initiated contact. And it nearly sent Brent over the edge as Scott held him tighter, clutching him. When Scott pulled away a little, Brent wasn't sure what he had in mind. Their eyes met and everything became perfectly clear. Scott leaned closer, parting his lips.

Brent held his breath, stilling. Scott needed to be the one to come the last distance. He wasn't going to push, no matter how much he wanted to. Scott came closer, hesitated, looking toward the kitchen door, then closed the distance between them.

Scott's lips were sweet, smooth, and hard, and he was one hell of a kisser. Where he'd learned was a mystery that Brent intended to solve, because he felt that kiss to his toes. Damn, he was on fire, and Scott became more insistent, getting carried away. Brent didn't want this to end, but he placed his hand gently on Scott's shoulder and patted him a few times to get his attention. Scott backed up, eyes dancing, lips curling into a grin. He looked toward the door once more and then laughed. It was a joyous sound, and maybe it meant that Scott had let go of some of his hurt, at least for a while.

Carolyn swept into the room, and Scott blinked as he looked up at her. Brent hoped what they'd just done wasn't written all over his face.

"Everything is fine, Mom. I'm okay. You can stop worrying now." He sat back. "I'm tired, but I'm not an invalid and I've been resting for most of the day."

"Scott is fine," Reggie said from behind her. "Come on. Let's you and I go for a walk down to the park. You could use some fresh air. I think Scott and Brent will be okay here for a while." He flashed Scott a smile.

"It's all right," Brent said, turning to Scott and picking up the pad. *I should go so you can rest. But please come down to the garage for a visit. I know that everyone there would very much like to see you.* He basked in the glow of Scott's gaze. Brent was fairly sure Reggie was offering to take Carolyn out of the house so they could have a few minutes to talk alone, but from her nervousness, she wasn't too happy about it. Though he didn't think she objected to him and Scott figuring out if there was anything between them. Brent hoped Carolyn was just being a protective mother.

"Watch a movie with me," Scott offered. "I use the subtitles, but it gives me something to do that feels normal. That is unless you really have to go somewhere." He seemed miserable, and Brent wasn't going to leave him alone.

He nodded. "We can watch whatever you like," Brent said, forgetting Scott's deafness for a moment.

"We'll go for that walk, and I'll make you some popcorn when we get back," Carolyn said.

Brent made sure Scott understood the plan, then sat back as Scott found a movie and placed it in the DVD player. Carolyn and Reggie left the room, and soon the back door opened and closed. He and Scott were alone, and Brent slipped a hand into his.

"You know, we could do more than watch a movie," Scott said. Brent reached for the notepad, but Scott stilled him. "I hate those things and the fact that no one can talk to me without one. I can't sit here and whisper things with you."

Brent nodded and waited until Scott reached for the notepad. *But you're still healing, and I think we need to spend some time together outside of work.*

"Don't you want to be with me?" Scott asked, speaking fast and more loudly.

Brent wrote quickly. *Of course I do. I stayed away all that time because... I thought it was the right thing to do. You have your whole life ahead of you, and I'm quite a bit older.* Sometimes he felt like an old man.

Scott caught his gaze, staring into him. "I'm not a kid, and I know my own mind." The words were harsh, but then his expression softened. "Do you still think I have my whole life ahead of me? Sometimes I wonder what kind of life I can have now." He lowered his head. "Working on cars is as much about sound as it is about what things look like. I honestly don't know how I can do my job. I know it's possible—I've seen how Lee works—but it's hard to imagine right now." He scratched the side of his head near the bandages. "I hate these things. They say they'll take them off on my next visit. Apparently it's a precaution, but they make my head itch sometimes."

Maybe it's your hair growing back.

"Probably. I got a look at myself in the mirror when they were changing the bandages. I look awful."

Brent smiled and leaned closer to scribble on the pad that Scott looked amazing no matter what, then gently kissed the base of his neck. Scott tasted of warmth, salty and yet slightly sweet at the same time. Scott groaned deep in his throat, a sound Brent was certain was involuntary. When he shifted back, Brent glanced to Scott's lap, the prominent bulge unmistakable and enticing.

"Do you see me as breakable?" Scott asked.

Brent shook his head.

"Then, we're alone and…." Scott drew out the last word, letting it hang in the air.

Brent was growing to hate the notepad as well. The words were flat, when what he wanted to say and the words he needed to use could carry so much meaning. So instead he took Scott's hand and placed it on his thigh, letting Scott see his excitement as well. He closed his eyes as a wave of heat jolted right through him just from that simple touch. Brent had longed for this for two years, and his entire being screamed out for him to take what Scott was offering. Brent's heart raced, blood pounding in his ears. He wondered if Scott would feel the same sensation. There were many things he wondered about.

You're recovering. He gently traced one of the bandages on Scott's head. *I will not hurt you.*

"But if you're careful."

Brent grinned and grabbed the pad. *When I am finally with you in bed and have you under my body and am able to feel all of you, every inch that I've dreamed of and fantasized about for years, I won't be able to contain myself. I want you... all of you.* Brent could hardly believe he was writing all this down. He looked up from the page, Scott's intense gaze boring into him. *I want to make you scream even if you can't hear it, and I want you to shake and shiver as I fill you. I want you to cling to me with everything you have as I hold you as tightly as I can, not letting an inch of space come between us.* Brent swallowed hard as he wrote and said the words in unison. He ripped off the page and handed it to Scott, whose hands shook as he read it, eyes widening, peering over the page, licking his lips, and swallowing hard.

"Brent, I…." His lips continued moving even if he made no sound, and Brent leaned close to capture them in a kiss that seared its way through him. Scott wrapped his arms around Brent's neck, pulling them tight, their kiss deepening to black-hole depths, threatening to swallow them both in an instant. Brent was seconds away from letting it happen.

He pulled back and then gently smoothed his hand across Scott's rough cheek. They needed to slow down, because Brent's control was becoming tenuous. He stood, tempted to tug Scott to his feet, take him by the hand, and lead him down the hall to his bedroom. But that wasn't in the cards, not for tonight. Brent had to cool down. He motioned to the television.

"You want to watch the movie?" Scott asked, in disbelief.

Brent snatched the paper off the table. *It's either that or I'm going to have my way with you, and when your mom and dad come home, they'll know exactly what we've been doing.* Brent stifled a smile at Scott's blushing cheeks. He dropped the pad, turned on the television, and handed Scott the remote so they could go ahead and watch *Rogue One*.

"I know this movie pretty well." The subtitles were on, and Scott settled back to watch. Brent sat on one end of the sofa so

Scott could have the rest, but soon Scott shifted to nestle up against him, lying down as he watched.

By the time Carolyn and Reggie returned, it was nearly dark outside and Scott's breathing had evened out. Brent suspected he was asleep.

"Did you have a good talk?" Carolyn asked.

"Yes." Brent didn't go into anything more than that. He folded the pages they'd written and placed them in his pocket. What they'd talked about was between the two of them, and Brent wanted Scott to be able to trust him. "Did you have a good walk?"

She nodded. "I think it was what I needed. A chance to get out of here and relax for a while." She leaned on the frame of the doorway to the kitchen. "I'll make some popcorn." Carolyn left, and Brent wondered if that was necessary. But as soon as the scent wafted into the room, Scott's eyes fluttered open and he sat up, licking his lips.

Carolyn brought in a huge bowl of popcorn and set it on the table. She returned with a couple sodas and some napkins. Before she'd left the room, Scott plopped the popcorn bowl onto his chest and started eating. "If you want some, you better get it while the getting is good," Carolyn warned him as Scott steadily dug into the popcorn. Brent would have sworn Scott had been starving for days.

Brent took some and popped a few kernels in his mouth as Scott returned his attention to the screen and absently shoveled the popcorn.

When the bowl was about half gone, Brent snatched it off Scott's belly and set it on his lap. Scott stretched for it, but Brent held the bowl out of his reach. "What gives?"

Brent set the bowl away and grabbed the pad. *You got yours and now this is my part.* He ate slowly, and Scott gaped at him.

"I usually eat that much alone."

Piggy? Brent scrawled and tossed the notepad at Scott. Then he returned to his share of the popcorn, this time not stopping Scott as he stole handfuls. At least Scott wasn't eating like the house was on fire.

"Do you mind if we change the film?" Scott asked, and Brent motioned for him to do what he wanted. He was just happy to sit with him and have someone to spend some time with. Scott changed the DVD to *The Man Who Knew Infinity*, and Brent quickly became engrossed in the story of an early twentieth-century math genius. Scott sat up and then leaned against him as they finished off the popcorn and their sodas.

By the time the movie ended, it was late. Brent thanked Reggie and Carolyn for everything as he brought the dishes to the kitchen. Then he returned to where Scott waited for him on the sofa and kissed him gently.

This was the best first date I've had in years, Brent wrote, handed the pad to Scott, then kissed him again and headed out to his car.

He drove back to his apartment, smiling the entire way. As he went inside and was locking the door, his phone chimed.

Good night and thank you. It was a wonderful evening. :)

Yes, it was. Maybe we can do it again sometime. When you're feeling better, you can come here. Brent thought what that kind of evening would bring and closed his eyes, letting his imagination run wild with images of what Scott might look like under his clothes. Brent had a pretty fertile imagination, but it failed him this time. He couldn't image Scott naked because he didn't want to guess—he wanted the reality more than anything else.

I was hoping we could do something on Sunday when the garage is closed. Even if it's just going to breakfast.

The words made Brent smile. *That would be wonderful.* He set his phone on the nightstand and undressed, getting ready for bed. He'd stayed up way too late and needed to be to work early, but he didn't regret a second of the best evening he'd had in a long time.

CHAPTER 4

SCOTT WOKE from a sound sleep to the scent of bacon. His stomach growled, and he rolled over to check the clock. It was before eight on Sunday and that meant his mother would be making her full-on breakfast, with enough food for a week. He pushed back the covers, got out of bed, and pulled on shorts and a T-shirt before wandering out to the kitchen.

"I have breakfast plans this morning."

His mother set down her spatula and turned, glaring at him with the wrath of God. "Church," she mouthed. Scott was able to read a few words, especially when he expected them.

"I'm not going." He turned away, but his mother caught his shoulder.

"Yes, you are." She pointed to a chair. He knew the drill. If you live under our roof... and all that. She got a pad. *They have a mass at nine that is signed for the deaf. It will do you good to go. There are other deaf members of the parish, and it would be good for you to meet them.*

Scott knew she was trying to help, but it made him angry nonetheless. He had no intention of stepping back into a church with the holier-than-thous. He crossed his arms over his chest, glaring at her, and then left the room. He had plans and wasn't going to change them. Scott dressed and got ready to go.

As he stepped out of the bedroom, his father was waiting. "Are you here to make me go?" Scott asked more harshly than he intended.

His dad shook his head. "You are an adult." His dad spoke slowly, but Scott shrugged, so his dad searched for a pad. Scott barely managed to contain his frustrated sigh. He grabbed one from his room and waited for his father to write what he wanted.

Your mother never asks you for very much, and she's been up for an hour so none of us will be late. He tore the page from the notebook and turned to walk away.

Damn it all. Scott hated when they used guilt on him. He groaned and got his phone from his room to text Brent to see if they could have lunch instead of breakfast. He explained what was happening and why he was going. To his shock Brent asked which church and agreed to meet them there.

I want to meet the interpreter, as well as the others, so I can better understand you.

The text had Scott gasping in disbelief.

You're going to come to church with me? Voluntarily? Are you really that wonderful or just plain crazy? Scott had to ask. He hated church, and now he was going to have to sit in a pew while everything happened around him. Just because they had a mass that was signed didn't mean anything. He didn't understand sign language, so it wasn't going to do him the least bit of good. Instead, he was going to be sitting there, cut off from everything and everyone, waiting for the ordeal to be over.

Let's go with crazy.

Scott smiled and messaged him the church and the time.

I'll meet you there.

Instantly Scott felt better about this whole ordeal and went to change.

He returned to the kitchen and ate some breakfast, but he wasn't really all that hungry—to his mother's clear disappointment. Scott hoped that he and Brent would still have some sort of plans, maybe for lunch, and he didn't want to fill up too much. After eating, they all got into the family Buick, with his father driving, and headed to church.

Scott sat in the back seat, staring as familiar homes and streets passed outside the car. The silence seemed overwhelming a lot of the time, and there was nothing he could do but try to fill his own head with his voice. He was getting tired of it.

The ride didn't take long—nothing was very far away in this densely populated community—and they pulled into their usual spot. Scott told his mom and dad that he was waiting for Brent and would be in. Then he stood off to the side of the main doors, waving at people he knew as they passed. The congregation was huge, with four masses on Sundays and one on Saturday evenings just to meet the demand.

Scott recognized Brent's old car when it pulled into the lot, and then followed Brent with his eyes as he got out and approached. He cleaned up well in simple dress pants and a white shirt that flowed over his lean muscles like water. It was open at the collar, and as Brent got closer, the strip of skin from his neck down to the gap in the shirt flashed and glowed in the sun. Scott couldn't move. Others passed in front of him, but Scott ignored them as mere shadows. His smile radiated light rivaling the sun's, big enough for the edges to extend to the corners of his eyes. When Brent reached him, he stopped and nodded. Someone jostled Scott from behind, and he took a step forward to balance himself. Brent caught him, holding him up as he turned.

Scott regained his balance, following Brent's gaze. "Martin and his wife, Cruella, I mean Gail. Part of the holier-than-thou clique," Scott explained, hoping he wasn't speaking too loudly.

"Bastard."

That Scott clearly understood as it crossed Brent's lips.

"This is supposed to be a church."

Scott caught that as well.

He rolled his eyes. "We used to be friends, the whole group of us. We were in youth group together for a little while. They were older by a few years. But as soon as I came out, they started making trouble because they think they're better than me."

Brent grabbed one of the small pads he always seemed to have handy. Maybe he bought them in bulk? *Did you catch what he said?*

Scott shook his head, but he could imagine.

What a jerk. Brent put the pad back into his pocket, motioning them toward the door. Scott walked with him and led Brent into the large sanctuary to the pew where his parents usually sat. He slid in and Brent sat next to him.

"Turn around when you get a chance. Three rows back is the rest of that group. Marshall, Spencer, and Louie."

Brent reached for a pad, but Scott stilled his hand. He knew what Brent was going to ask, but he wasn't going to have this particular conversation here. There were too many busybody eyes and ears.

Scott placed his hands on the pew ahead of them as the organ started playing. He could feel the vibrations of the sound through the building, but that was all. After the song ended and everyone stood for the start of the service, Scott stayed sitting where he was. His mother nudged him, but he was making a point. This held no meaning for him any longer, and he wasn't some robot to go through the motions. He touched his ribs, and his mother turned away, leaving him alone.

Never in his life had Scott been so surrounded by people and yet utterly alone. The congregation stood and sat, the organ played, processions and mysticism went on through the sanctuary, but none of it was for him. He watched the signer for a while, fascinated by her hand movements but not understanding any of them.

Scott studied the stained glass windows. Those he had always loved. They were part of the older church that had stood on the site years ago. When the building had been no longer viable, the early twentieth-century windows were removed and incorporated into the new building. He knew those images so very well, with their stunningly bright colors. Familiar stories came to mind, and he let them play through his head, paying little attention to anything else around him other than when Brent gently touched his shoulder every now and then. There was one person here who had come especially for him.

At one point everyone filed out of the pews for communion. He and Brent stayed behind, waiting for his parents to return. At least that signaled the near end of the service.

Thankfully, after a few more minutes of silence and boredom, it was over. Scott stood and carefully made his way out of the pew. His ribs ached and he wished he'd stayed at home. His seat had been at the exact wrong angle, and holding himself still caused pressure on the muscles of his chest and belly. He turned to Brent, who mouthed, "I know" and took his arm, gently guiding him toward the back, where everyone filed out. His parents greeted the priest at the door. Scott passed through without a look in his direction. All he wanted was to get to a car and then home so he could lie down.

"Dammit," he cursed, hoping it was under his breath.

Brent patted his shoulder and helped him out of the church. As soon as the bright sunshine hit his skin, Scott felt Brent tense, then walk a little faster. He turned to see what was going on, and his mother and father stared back from the door, where Spencer stood, glaring at him.

"What did he say?" Scott asked.

His mother paled, and his dad's face was red. He'd only seen him that way a few times in his life, and those instances were always before a giant explosion.

"Let's get out of here," Scott said as levelly as he could. "I need to rest awhile." He had hoped he'd be up to doing lunch with Brent, but that seemed like a stretch now.

The drive home was quiet. Scott went inside and sat on the sofa, not even bothering to take off his shoes. As soon as he lay down, the muscles relaxed and the soreness dissipated. He figured it was mostly fatigue and closed his eyes, letting that morning slip away as best he could.

He cracked his eyes as weight settled on the sofa next to him. From the rich scent that surrounded him, he knew it was Brent. "You want to know what all that was about?"

Brent nodded and waited. Thankfully, he didn't reach for one of those damned pads.

"I told you we were in youth group together. Spencer is the leader of that little group, and at one of the sleepovers—lock-ins we called them—he and I were up later than the others and, well…. He gave every indication that he wanted to… you know." God, he hoped he was being quiet enough that his mom and dad didn't hear. "I went to the bathroom, and he followed me in. Then he kissed me. One of the other boys was in the stall, but we didn't know because we were too stupid to look. Anyway, we'd been caught, and Spencer told everyone that I came on to him and forced him. It was ugly. The big closet case."

Out came one of those pads. *The others believed him?*

Scott nodded, wishing he could disappear. "They all guessed I was gay, I guess, so that went along with their views, and Spencer got to keep his reputation. Ever since, I've been this dirty guy and they act like they're perfect. Three of the four are married, and Spencer is supposedly dating one of the girls at church, but who knows if that's for real or not. They volunteer and participate in committees and boards—all things to make themselves look productive and useful." He sighed. "I don't want to dismiss what they do, because they do things other people don't want to do and they give of their time and shit. But it's the attitude like they're better than me."

Your mom and dad heard it. Have they done that before? Brent asked.

Scott nodded. "Yeah. That was how I came out. It was a shock to them, I think." His parents understood and had been supportive, believing him when he told them what happened.

But him being gay and their beliefs tended to have a weekly clash that revolved around church. "This is one area that causes conflict between us."

I can see that. Brent patted his hand after showing him his message. *I should head home and let you rest.*

"You don't want to go to lunch?" Scott asked. The last thing he wanted was to spend the rest of the day at home doing nothing. It would make his mother happy, but he was dying of boredom. "If I rest a few minutes, I'll be all right." He carefully stretched, blaming those awful church seats for his soreness.

If you're sure. Brent moved to a nearby chair.

Scott's mother bustled in nervously. She brought them both something to drink, her face redder than usual.

"It's okay, Mom. They're jerks." This wasn't her fault, but that whole going to church thing was off the table. He was done, and now he had plenty of ammunition. His mom and dad could continue to go if they wanted; that was their choice, but he wasn't. Scott slowly sat up to drink the juice she'd brought him, then rested a few minutes. "Brent and I are going to go to lunch."

She gave him that "is that a good idea?" look most mothers have.

"I'm going to be fine. The pew bothered me. That's all."

His father joined them. Scott got the idea that they wanted to talk and that twenty questions was about to begin. The only thing was, Scott wasn't interested, and shut them out simply by closing his eyes. Yeah, it was a little childish, but stuff like this had been going on for a while now and they'd seemed to ignore it before. But now they were all up in arms, and he wanted it to go away.

He knew Brent was speaking with his mom, and he tried to think of how he felt about that. His mom and dad spoke about him all the time now. They thought he didn't notice the way they talked even when he was in the room. One thing he'd learned was what his name looked like when it was being said, and he saw it quite a bit. Maybe it was natural for people to talk when deaf people were present, but it sometimes made him feel like he wasn't there. What surprised him was how he didn't feel that way with Brent. Sure, they were probably talking about him, but Brent had his back. At least Scott thought he did.

When Scott opened his eyes again, Brent was still sitting in the chair across from him, but his mother had left the room. *I reassured your mother that I would make sure you took it easy this afternoon and didn't do anything strenuous.* The wicked smile on his lips promised just the opposite.

Scott wanted to close his eyes again just to block out the crush of ravenous thoughts that raced through his head. But, damn, he wasn't able to. Brent leaned forward just a little, and Scott's breath left his chest. He didn't need words to read the heat in Brent's eyes. He could see the way he licked his lips, slowly, purposefully, letting him see just the hint of pink tongue.

He'd been with a few guys. Heck, Scott wasn't exactly a virgin, but he wasn't the most experienced guy either. A few dates, some fumbling, but mostly things hadn't worked out, and sometimes things… well, they'd blown up in his face. Brent made him want to push that aside.

Scott sat up slowly, testing his chest and back muscles. He felt better. He took Brent's hand, and they walked through to the kitchen. "Mom, Brent and I are going to go. I won't be out late, and I'll text if anything happens. I promise." He let go and hugged his mom goodbye, taking a deep breath. Being angry and upset with her wasn't going to solve anything.

Brent and his mom talked briefly, and then they left the house. Instantly Scott could breathe again as some of the tension drained away. "Mom and Dad watch me all the time like I'm going to break."

Brent nodded.

"I know they mean well, but I'm not a baby."

Brent tossed the pad at him. *You're their baby, and nothing is ever going to change that.*

Scott carefully climbed into the car, made sure his seat belt was fastened, and as Brent pulled away, continually scanned the area for other cars. He'd been doing that a lot since the accident and hoped the need would die away soon. He wanted to be comfortable in his own life, but that was probably quite a ways off.

The drive to Brent's apartment didn't take long, and once there, Brent unlocked the door to let him in. It was plain, but the furniture looked comfortable, lived in. This was Brent's home and it felt like it. Everything was for use, not just for show, just like Mom and Dad's. "This is nice."

"It's home."

Scott liked how Brent always made a point of looking at him when he spoke and did it slower so he'd have a chance to understand. "I like it."

Brent motioned to the sofa and went into the kitchen. He began pulling things out, and Scott realized Brent intended to cook for him. He wasn't sure, but judging by the fact that Brent usually ordered a sandwich each day at work from the local Cousins Subs, he figured cooking wasn't something Brent did a lot of. He held up a bag of pasta, and Scott nodded. Brent got things going and then dug up the remote control.

"Shit," Brent said, turning on the television and reprogramming it so the closed captioning came up. Then he handed the remote to Scott with a smile. *Tell me more about these jerks in church*, Brent wrote, then went back to his cooking. The rooms were open, so it didn't seem as though Brent was very far away.

"I told you most of it. We used to be friends."

But who cares what happened, then? Brent wrote quickly.

"I wish I knew. Spencer is obviously so deep in the closet, he can barely think for all the clothes between him and the door. I think his family would freak out from one end of the county to the other if they thought he was gay, so he hides it and then makes my life, and anyone else who's out, miserable so no one would suspect him." Scott snickered. "He was also a lousy kisser, and from what I heard from one of the girls in church, that particular trait hasn't changed. Linda used the term 'kissing a dead fish' to describe him. And she probably has it about right."

Brent made a face, and Scott laughed again. *Just leave and don't go back.*

"That's what I intend to do. I have to tell Mom and Dad that I'm not going back. They won't be happy. The church is such a huge portion of their social life, and it used to be mine. But not anymore. It doesn't feel safe any longer, and now that I can't hear, it's like sitting in a room full of people who have shut you out and won't let you in on the secret. There's nothing I want there, so I'm going to say goodbye to them. I need to find my own path, and they aren't on it with me." Scott sighed in relief. He felt so much better just saying what he intended to do to someone.

Brent continued working and let Scott ramble on. He talked about all kinds of stuff, most of it unimportant, but Brent seemed to pay attention, asking some questions occasionally.

Have the police found out anything else?

"No. I think they're giving up and moving on to other things. They haven't said so, but I know they're busy."

Brent frowned and picked up the notepad. *Text me the kind of car involved. I can ask Trevor to check with his shops and some others to see if anyone has brought in that kind of car for front-end repair.* He set down the notepad and picked up a knife.

"Do you really think that will help?" Scott asked. That sounded like grasping at straws to him.

Brent shrugged and set down his knife to walk through the apartment to the door. He opened it, and a guy about Brent's age swaggered in but stopped on a dime as soon as he saw Scott. The guy was as tall as Brent, thin, and poured into a pair of jeans that were a decade too young for him. He set down the six-pack he was carrying, and he and Brent talked briefly. Then Brent went back to the pad.

This is Dean, a friend of mine and Trevor's, Brent wrote, and Scott shook his hand.

Dean started talking what looked like a mile a minute, gesturing with his hands and smiling. He seemed excited to meet Scott, which was good, but of course Scott had no idea what he was saying. Brent tossed Dean the pad, and he wrote frantically.

When he turned the note around, a couple of things struck Scott. First, that Dean had the handwriting of a doctor, and second, that he was truly as excited as he looked. *Brent has been talking about you for months and months. It's great to finally meet you.* He took the pad back, scribbled, and gave it to Scott again. *I'm sorry about your accident and all. I hope things get better soon.* He tugged back the pad and flipped the page. *Brent says he's going to take sign language classes. I think that's cool.*

"So do I." Scott turned to Brent, who seemed to find all this as fascinating as he did. "Brent has been great since the accident, and we're starting to figure some things out."

I hope so. He's been pining for you forever. He and I used to go out to the clubs and things, but we haven't done that a lot lately. Mainly because of you.

"Is that bad?" Scott asked, and Brent grinned and shook his head. Brent pulled out a bottle of wine, motioning to him. Scott shook his head. "I'm still on pain medication, so I can't drink."

Brent poured himself a glass and brought Scott a Coke. Then he sat down next to him, and he and Dean had a talk. Once again, Scott knew people were talking about him, but he sat back, close to Brent, feeling at ease.

Dean grabbed the pad from the table. *I think Brent is falling for you.* Dean got this shit-eating grin on his face, and Brent reached across and smacked Dean hard, clearly yelling at him. *Apparently I'm an ass.*

"You might be if you think something like that is a joking matter. Whatever Brent feels for me, it's up to him to tell me, not you." Scott understood Brent's frustration, feeling it rolling off him.

Brent whacked Dean with the notepad, but that seemed good-natured, and wrote. *Dean has complete diarrhea of the mouth. He tends to run on without a damned off switch. One day his big mouth is going to get him into trouble.* He put his arm around Scott, tugging him a little closer. *I need to finish making lunch.* Brent took the pad with him as he went back to the kitchen.

"Do you have any stories you can tell me about Brent?" Scott asked.

Dean nodded, grinning from ear to ear. Scott suspected Brent was protesting from where he was working, but judging by his expression, he seemed okay. Dean grabbed a notebook that Brent must have put on the table in anticipation of him coming over and began to write.

I could tell you something stupid, like the time we went camping and he left the cooler of food sitting back home near the door of his place. It was his idea to spend some time in nature, but instead we stayed at a Best Western before coming back home to civilization. Scott laughed as he read that. *But I want to say that Brent is one of the best guys I have ever met and I hope you treat him well. He deserves to be happy, and he has been lately. You seem to make him happy. So don't hurt him!* The last sentence was underlined three times.

"I'll do my best not to." Scott couldn't see into the future, but he didn't set out to hurt anyone.

He sat back, getting comfortable, watching Brent work in the kitchen. He obviously wasn't a practiced cook. His motions were careful rather than fluid and familiar. Still, the scent of tomatoes and garlic filled the room, making Scott's mouth water.

Dean wrote and then turned to the television.

Brent said to tell you that he has a pecan pie from his mother for dessert.

Scott alternated between watching them, wondering if Dean was planning to stay for the duration. Scott thought this was supposed to have been some time for them together, but Dean seemed settled in, and Brent wasn't telling him to leave. Maybe this was just some time away from his family and not the date that Scott had thought it was.

"Are you making fresh sauce?" he asked.

Brent shook his head. "Mom."

Scott's hunger increased. If her sauce was anything like her pie, he was in for a treat.

Dean began talking to Brent once again and then stood up. He waved goodbye, and Scott shook his hand once again.

"It was nice to meet you."

"You too," Dean said and headed for the door, taking his beer with him. Brent showed him out, closing the door, then leaned against it dramatically.

"Does he come over like that often?"

Brent grabbed a pad, and Scott looked forward to not having to have everyone write shit down all the time. It was driving him crazy.

Brent came over and tossed the pad onto the table. *Sometimes. He's feeling adrift right now. Recovering from a bad boyfriend and breakup. He's screwed a bunch of guys, but he's lonely and wants to try to find someone, but doesn't know how.*

Brent leaned in, and Scott's temperature rose through the roof in a matter of seconds. Brent hadn't even touched him and Scott's skin ached for it. Brent came closer, pressing their lips together. Scott wound his arms around Brent's neck, holding him tighter, deepening the kiss. He was hungrier for Brent than he was for the amazing food whose scent called to him like a siren song.

"Eat?"

Scott pulled him closer once again, humming softly to himself as he tugged Brent down onto the sofa. He felt rumbles run through Brent's chest and realized he was laughing. Scott pulled away, glaring at him. "Am I funny? Do I kiss funny?"

Brent cradled his cheeks in his hands, looking deeply into Scott's eyes without the hint of a smile. All he saw was heat mixed with care. Scott tried to imagine what it would be like to go to bed seeing those eyes and then wake up each morning, seeing them again before anything else. As soon as the notion crossed his mind, Scott dismissed it as ridiculous. Yes, Brent was being kind to him now. But if his hearing never returned— and in Scott's mind, that was becoming more and more likely— then he was going to need assistance for the rest of his life in one way or another. It was easy enough for Brent to say he was going to take signing classes, but two years was the minimum for the basics. Fluency took years, and somehow he didn't see a guy like Brent—handsome, strong, hot as all hell—going through that for a guy like him.

Brent reached for the pad and wrote a quick note. *What's the matter? I saw the shadow pass over your eyes.*

Scott shook his head. "Just a dose of reality."

Whatever Brent said, Scott didn't catch, but he stroked his cheeks, leaned closer, and kissed him hard enough to short-circuit Scott's thought processes for a week. Scott caught his breath, returning the kiss, holding Brent as close as he dared with his sore ribs, and letting go of his reservations. He was on fire, burning up, and he needed relief, but Brent wasn't providing any. Second by second, the heat built until Scott closed his eyes and allowed himself to just feel.

When Brent pulled away, Scott slid his eyes open to find Brent looking back at him intently, as though he were the only other person on earth.

"What happens when you get tired of being with someone who can't hear?" Scott asked. "I know I'm talking, but I can't even hear myself. Mom makes these motions when I talk too loud and—"

Brent cupped his chin gently and didn't move his lips. Instead, he stared at him until Scott began to squirm. He looked away, and Brent reached behind him to get a pad.

So you can't hear. Do you think that's the worst thing in the world? Deaf people are incredibly independent. Yes, they sometimes have communication challenges, but we will work through those. He shook the pad and wrote again. *If I have to buy up every notepad in town, I will.*

"But it's so hard and…." He swallowed as Brent nodded, and a spike of fear raced through him. Was Brent agreeing with him that it was hard for him too?

No. It's pretty easy. Being around you is easy. I don't feel like I have to be anyone but me. Brent seemed surprised, and he slowly set down the pad, looking back at him. Then he grabbed it again. *My mom always said that the way she knew she loved my dad was because she could be herself with him. She didn't have to wear fancy clothes or put on tons of makeup. He liked her the way she came, and that's how I like you. As you are.* He handed Scott the notebook and held up one finger before leaving the room.

Scott sat back, watching Brent head toward the bathroom, wondering what had just happened. He went over the conversation, reading the note again. Then he smiled as the full potential of those words sank in.

When Brent came back out, he went right to the kitchen, working on lunch once again.

"Did you mean it?" Scott asked. "Or was that something you said and it got out of hand?"

Brent had pulled out a head of lettuce and was cutting it up. His knife came to a stop and he looked up from what he was doing. "I meant it," he said slowly, then returned to what he'd been doing.

Scott stood and walked to where Brent was sliding the lettuce into a bowl and cutting up a tomato. "If that's true, then why are you more interested in vegetables than looking at me?"

Brent stopped once again. He reached for a pad. *I wasn't expecting to say anything. Sometimes things happen really fast and they surprise you. I think that's what happened to me. Isn't it too soon for me to be telling you stuff like that?* Fear rose in Brent's eyes as he wrote.

"What are you afraid of?"

Brent snatched the pad off the counter and wrote again. Then he handed the page to Scott and frantically worked to finish lunch. Scott read the note, glancing at Brent and then back at the words, almost unable to believe them. "What do you mean, that you might not be good enough?" He tossed the pad on the counter, trying to process what might be behind them. But he wasn't getting anywhere. This was a side of Brent he hadn't seen, and it took him a little by surprise. Brent had been pursuing him, supporting and helping, and now all of a sudden, he was stepping back in a way that Scott didn't understand.

Brent reached for the pad. *It's not important.* He held up the sign, then motioned Scott around and dipped a spoon into the sauce for him to taste. This was clearly a way to pull the conversation from what had just happened. Scott was still deciding if he was going to allow himself the distraction when the spicy richness hit his mouth. The sauce was as incredible as it smelled, and Scott hummed in his throat. He couldn't hear it, but he could feel it, and at least he knew he was making some sort of sound to show his pleasure. Scott swallowed and nodded. It was truly delicious. That was the only word that came to mind.

But once the taste had slipped away and the intensity faded, he still looked at Brent. Something was going on; Scott could feel it. Brent bit his lower lip, and if Scott wasn't mistaken, nervous energy had replaced the easy camaraderie they'd had not too long before.

Scott pulled up the stool from next to the stove and sat at the end of the counter. This was so frustrating, and he wanted to be able to get to the bottom of what was happening with Brent.

And if Brent was going to try to hide or pull back, there was nothing he could do about it. It felt like part of Scott's heart had been cut away as Brent distanced himself.

It would have been so easy before. He'd have simply asked Brent again, and then they might have gone to the sofa or Scott would have pulled an explanation out of him and listened. But things were different now. Just like that, what might have carried the weight of sadness or gravity were now simply words on a flat sheet of paper. That was what really sucked. And Brent had to be feeling it too. No wonder he didn't want to talk about whatever was bothering him. It wasn't as though Scott could feel the hurt in Brent's voice.

Maybe what Brent needed was to talk about this with Dean. At least they could listen to each other. Scott watched Brent like a hawk, as though he could divine some important revelation from his body language, but all he got was that something was bothering him. He saw it in the way Brent's back was so straight and his movements forced and choppy.

"Did I do something?" Scott asked. God, he hoped not.

Brent shook his head, but it didn't have any impact on Scott. There must have been something that made Brent feel this way, and the only person in the room at the time was him, so therefore he must be the cause.

Scott gripped the edge of the counter nervously, wondering if he should ask Brent to take him home instead of getting angry. "I'm still here, Brent," he spat angrily. It was so easy for others to cut him out now. Brent reached for the pad, but Scott stopped his hand. "You need to talk to me. I know it's hard because I can't hear." He huffed and wanted to smack the counter. He released Brent's hand, and Brent took the pad.

This has nothing to do with you not being able to hear. Brent underlined "nothing" a bunch of times. *It's just me, and there are some things I need to work through.* Brent paused with the pen hovering over the paper.

"Are you afraid? Of me?" Scott found that hard to believe.

Brent turned away, pulled the pasta off the stove, and drained the water in the sink. Then he added the sauce and stirred it together. Scott waited until he was done, knowing there was nothing he could do until Brent decided to write another note. It was frustrating. He could talk all he wanted, but he couldn't make Brent answer him. Brent dished up two plates and carried them to the small table, then brought the salad and the rest of lunch.

"Are you going to talk to me?" Scott's frustration rose by the second, and he was probably yelling but didn't care. "I'm tired of being cut out and passed over. My parents do it, but I didn't think you would."

I'm not, Brent wrote. He laid the pad on the table, then turned it around. *I'm a coward, okay?*

"No, you're not," Scott breathed.

You don't know, Brent scrawled and sat down. *You're scared that I might get tired of you or something, so why can't I be afraid that I'm not good enough for you?*

Scott didn't have an answer to that, and it made him feel better in some perverse way that Brent was scared too. Since he'd awakened in the hospital, Scott had been living with constant fear. Was his hearing going to come back? And then, when Brent seemed interested in him, was Brent going to stick around or was he going to get tired of him? Scott certainly hoped he didn't, but knowing Brent was afraid as well put them on more equal footing.

"I always thought of you as a really confident guy," Scott said. "You run the garage like you were born to it, and all the guys like and respect you. They listen to you. I never thought you were a coward, not for a second."

There are things you don't know.

Brent stood and got the salt and pepper before rejoining him at the table. They began eating. It seemed strange to leave the conversation where they had, but Scott was getting used to conversations ending weirdly, because it sometimes took so much effort to maintain them.

"Then maybe you should tell me." That seemed like a real cop-out to him, but Brent closed his eyes and shook his head, withdrawing further. Clearly this was a no-go area for him. "You don't have to." It wasn't like he had told Brent every single thing about himself either. And a person deserved some privacy if they wanted it. He reached across the table to take Brent's hand. "It really is okay. You'll talk about it when you're ready."

Brent nodded and made an effort at a smile, which was heartening to see. "I'm sorry for being a downer," Brent said twice. Scott understood it the second time.

"It's okay." He grinned. "It's nice to know we both have issues. If you were perfect, then I'd wonder about me."

Brent shook his head, clearly amused, and took the first bite of the farfalle pasta in meat sauce. Scott followed suit, and man, was it good. Rich tomato, garlic, onion, oregano. All the things that made life special. Scott's mother was a good cook, but Italian food, especially sauce, was doctored stuff out of the jar. It was good, but it didn't taste like tomato heaven.

Lunch was amazing, the food spectacular. They didn't talk about anything, mainly because their hands were otherwise occupied and it seemed ridiculous to try to pass notes back and forth. The earlier tension dissipated like fog against the summer sun, and things returned to how they were before.

"I wish I could tell you a joke." Scott used to love telling funny stories.

"Go ahead."

Scott shook his head. "It's one of those that requires input, and it wouldn't work out. I tried joking with my dad, and he looked at me like I'd grown a second head."

Brent reached for the damn pad. *Maybe there are deaf jokes. I mean, once you meet other deaf people, they'll have their own jokes and culture. I read that local communities often develop their own signing slang as a way of speaking to each other. I bet they have their own humor.*

"I read that too." Scott smiled as he swallowed his last bite of pasta and took a little more salad, very nearly full. "I'm really looking forward to meeting some people who can help me figure things out. I mean, I know I'm deaf and that my hearing isn't going to come back. I can feel it in my bones, and I have to be prepared for that."

You know you have a lot of us behind you.

He did, which was part of what made it easier to get up and face the day each morning. "I'm looking forward to seeing Lee again. I'm not sure how we'll work together, but I think we can work it through. He came to the house yesterday for a little while and we hung out. It wasn't the same as it was before, but we'll get it. He had his tablet and we were able to talk, so it was good. I'm not sure how things will go when we're at work."

Brent wrote, then handed him the pad and began clearing the dishes.

Lee will be your ears and you will be his eyes. The rest will sort itself out.

Scott ate the last bite of salad, and Brent took care of his plate before setting an amazing pecan pie on the table.

Do you want dessert now or later?

Scott rubbed his full belly and thought later was probably the smart choice. He stood, waving the pie off for now, and Brent got a couple of Cokes and joined him on the sofa.

"I never know what to do when we sit like this. Before I used to watch movies and play video games. I can still do both, but they're flat now. Half the time it isn't what's on the screen that makes a movie exciting, but the soundtrack. It's the spooky music that makes a horror movie fun or gives it the undercurrent of suspense that makes a tingle go up your spine. I can't hear any of that anymore. All I get is dialog on the screen and the occasional indication that music is playing. Even video games aren't as fun, because half the experience is the soundtrack."

What do you think we should do? Brent asked.

"We can watch a movie or television if you want. You turned on the closed captioning, so that will be fine."

Brent jumped to his feet. He showed him the pad. *I know. How about a walk?*

"I can't walk too far."

Brent pulled out the pad once again. *The park is a block away, and there are some wonderful things I want to show you.* He held out his hand, and Scott took it, letting Brent help him up. Brent then raced through the apartment, coming up with his keys and the things he needed. He met Scott at the door and led him down to the main entryway of the building.

The air outside was warm, the sun strong, the breeze making it perfect. Brent walked slowly, and Scott took careful steps, testing his muscles and finding the discomfort from earlier in the day was nowhere to be found. He walked a little faster, enjoying the time away from the confines of his mom and dad, and in Brent's company.

Brent pointed and Scott looked, watching a hawk as it circled in the air, riding the currents high above them. Before he might have heard it cry, but now he was content to watch it. "I need to learn to be grateful for what I have instead of longing for what's been taken."

Brent patted him on the hand, smiling, and nodded.

"Maybe I should have T-shirts printed."

Brent threw his head back and laughed so hard, his body trembled.

Maybe that wasn't such a bad idea.

They continued walking, with Brent holding his arm, the outward display of affection surprising and nice. A block from Brent's apartment, they entered a canopy of large trees, and in an instant, they were surrounded by coolness. "This is nice." He sighed and looked up, watching the sun play through the leaves, sending shafts of light to the grass under his shoes.

Brent pointed, and they headed in that direction. The path traveled through thick growth and then widened as a small creek passed next to it, the water cooling the air even further. It was amazing. Brent stopped and took out the pad. *We'll follow the path along the stream for a little ways.* He pointed, and Scott nodded, letting Brent guide the way.

After ten minutes, they came to a stop, and Scott sat on the end of an upturned log next to a small waterwheel that turned slowly in the current. "Is this what you wanted me to see?"

Brent nodded, already writing. *I used to play here when I was a kid. Our house, the one Mom still lives in, is a few blocks that way.* He pointed. *My dad used to bring me here all the time, and I'd play with the waterwheel and the creek, making raceways and dams that the water would wash away. It was magical.*

Scott could imagine that.

I was ten when the waterwheel broke, and my dad took it back to the garage and built a new one for me. Brent pointed again, and Scott realized that was the one he was looking at. *I don't know how much longer it will last, but it's turned for a lot of years now. Dad built it strong.* Brent put his arm around Scott, holding him close.

Scott held Brent in return, knowing instinctively it was what he needed. Whatever had been bothering Brent had to do with his dad. The more words he wrote about him, the sadder Brent had become. It didn't take a genius to know whatever had happened between the two of them bothered Brent greatly. Scott sat, watching the little wheel turn around and around. He imagined the sound of the water as it splashed over the edge.

Eventually Scott stood, gingerly stepped over the wet ground to the wheel, and placed his hands in the stream of water. It felt good, and he wriggled his fingers, getting them wet, then filled his hands and tossed the water at Brent, who jumped back. Scott grinned and did it again.

He had no idea what Brent said, but water flew at him, and Scott laughed, deep, full, and from his soul. For once he didn't care that he had no idea what he sounded like. All that mattered was having a little fun, and damn, he was happy. More water flew his way, and he splashed Brent in return, laughing like a complete idiot and having a good time.

Brent raced to him, and his arms encircled Scott's waist, holding him carefully.

Scott stood carefully, turning in Brent's embrace until he faced him. "It's beautiful here. Your dad helped make it that way."

Tears filled Brent's eyes as he nodded, and then Brent kissed him, holding him tight. Scott wound his arms around Brent, supporting him. The kiss was hot, toe-curling, but there was something under it, something deeper and more urgent. Need, care, companionship, and a void of compassion that begged to be filled. Those ideas filled Scott's head, and he tightened his hold, supporting Brent the way Brent had done for him.

Scott didn't want this to end, but his energy was fading quickly and he was going to need to lie down and probably take a pain pill. "We should walk back to your apartment. I'm really getting tired."

Brent shifted and gently led him away from the water, supporting part of his weight as he led him to the path and back the way they'd come. They walked slowly, and Scott was grateful when they reached the door to Brent's apartment.

Brent unlocked it and then guided him to the sofa. Scott lay down, closing his eyes, his tense muscles in his chest and back loosening up within seconds, the soreness fading quickly. Brent pressed a cold can into his hand, and Scott sipped the Coke, letting the coolness coat his parched throat.

"Thank you for taking me there." Scott sighed. "I can go home if you need me to leave."

The cushion next to him dipped, and Scott cracked his eyes open. Instantly the world brightened, and when Brent smiled, it was as if the sun came from behind a cloud. Scott had to smile in return. Brent slowly stroked his arm, soothing, caring, and surprisingly intimate.

"I take it you want me to stay?"

Brent nodded deliberately and leaned forward to kiss him firmly, stoking the fire that had simmered below the surface all afternoon. The flame flared to life in seconds. Unfortunately Scott was too tired to do anything about it. And he was afraid, if he were truthful. Getting excited was one thing, but his bones were still healing, and what if he injured something again? He didn't want to end up back in the hospital. Still, he returned the kiss, holding Brent because it felt amazing, and he didn't feel alone. Brent didn't make him feel as though he was on the outside looking in.

Brent's breath ghosted over his ear, and then he pulled away. *You rest for a while.* Brent patted Scott's arm, then stood, sat in the chair next to Scott's feet, and pulled a book up off the floor. He opened it, flashing a smile at Scott over the pages, and Scott took another drink of soda, then set the can on the table and closed his eyes again, letting sleep wash over him.

IT SURPRISED Scott that he felt comfortable enough to sleep. Since losing his hearing, he hadn't slept particularly well. Scott would have thought just the opposite, with no sounds to wake him, but he found he was more nervous than he expected and would bolt upright a few times during the night just to check what time it was. His mother had ordered an alarm clock that flashed lights instead of made noise, but that didn't do a lot of good for him, particularly if he happened to be facing the other way, so he woke himself up just so he wouldn't lose track of the time. Yeah, it sounded weird, but it was a way of compensating for having lost part of the way he functioned.

Scott opened his eyes and glanced around. Brent still sat in the chair, reading. Scott checked his watch, realizing he'd been asleep for an hour and that he felt better. He carefully sat up, and Brent stood, retrieved his soda from the refrigerator, and placed it back on the coaster on the coffee table.

"That was nice. Thank you."

Brent set the pad on the table and took a seat next to him. *You were tired and needed to rest. It was no problem. I want you to be happy.*

"I want to be happy, and I want that for you too." Scott leaned against Brent. It had been a while since he had been happy. Somehow the driver of the car that hit him had taken away his ability to be truly happy, as well as his hearing. And in Scott's mind, that needed to change. He couldn't give a nameless person that kind of power. If he did, then he'd never be able to move past this, and he didn't want to be unhappy for the rest of his life.

Scott leaned on Brent's shoulder and sighed, smiling as Brent stroked his cheek. He hadn't shaved in a few hours and his cheeks were most likely rough, but Brent didn't seem to mind. Brent turned his head slowly and then leaned in to kiss him.

His lips were gentle at first but became more demanding, the kiss deeper. Brent's tongue traced the outline of Scott's lips and then slid between them, taking possession. Scott leaned back, holding Brent in case he flew apart. Energy raced through him, and he held Brent tighter, returning the heat Brent sent to him measure for measure. He tried to hold still but failed as his entire body shook. His need for Brent grew by the second, and when Brent gently pressed him back onto the cushions, he went willingly, easily, clutching at Brent's back, trying to tug his shirt up and out of the way.

Brent lifted Scott's shirt, tugging the tails out of his pants, and then undid the buttons. He parted the fabric and pushed it to the side, baring Scott's chest to him for the first time. Brent kissed his belly and up his side, avoiding his recent scars. They were so sensitive and still a little raw. Though Brent did gently caress the puckered skin, he moved on, driving Scott crazy with his gentle caresses.

"I know I can't hear you. But just so you know, you're driving me crazy."

Brent raised his head, smiling wickedly, like he knew exactly what he was doing. Damn, Brent was beautiful. His eyes shone, and Scott caressed his cheeks, bringing his mouth closer to Brent's, closing the distance between them, bringing them together in a searing kiss. He slid his hands down Brent's back, tugged his shirt up until Brent pulled away, taking off his shirt, and then they were skin to skin, chest to chest, heat to heat.

Scott heard no words. He didn't need them. Brent made him feel alive, and being deaf didn't matter, because Brent cared for him. They didn't even have their pants off, and Scott was already flying, alive and excited beyond belief.

Brent lifted himself up to stand next to the sofa and extended his hand. Scott took it, and Brent led him to the bedroom and then down onto the bed, treating him as though he were precious. Brent didn't rush, but took his time, caressing Scott all over until he nearly set the sheets on fire. And when Brent did unfasten Scott's pants and tug them down his legs, Scott was so excited and ready, he nearly lost it just from the caress of Brent's hand on his inner thigh. He shook and whispered unsexy thoughts under his breath to keep himself from coming.

When Brent kicked off his shoes and then turned around, opened his pants, and pushed them down over his tight butt, Scott's control reached the breaking point. And when Brent faced him again, Scott bit his lower lip as Brent drew nearer.

Brent climbed on the bed, the heat between them growing with each movement. He tugged him closer, kissed him, and rolled on the bed so Scott rested on top of Brent, who held him tight, hands roaming over his back and down to his butt to clutch him.

"I never knew sex could be like this." Scott paused, their gazes locking, and words failed him.

Scott straddled Brent, holding him as their bodies moved together. Scott had to take it easy, but Brent matched him action for action as pressure built to the point where Scott could no longer contain it. He hadn't thought of himself as a teenager in a long time, but dammit, he felt like one at this moment. He was hard, tingly, and on the edge of a razor within seconds, and then tumbled over the other side with Brent following behind him, eyes and mouth wide open, ecstasy written all over his face, mirroring Scott's own.

Neither of them moved for a long while, reveling in the time for the two of them when the world didn't matter and nothing could touch them.

CHAPTER 5

THE FOLLOWING morning Brent made sure all the guys knew what they were supposed to be doing for the day. A rather tricky problem had come in first thing, and he put Lee and Clyde on it, hoping Lee's sensitive hearing would fish out the problem. Once he knew the guys were busy, he went to his office and began making calls. The first ones were to Trevor's other garages to make sure they hadn't worked on a car that met the description of the one that hit Scott.

"I already checked," Trevor's dad, Larry, said. "I've been on the lookout myself." Larry had married his girlfriend, Margaret, a year ago and was getting ready to retire and move to Florida.

"How are the move plans coming?"

"Awesome," Larry said, sounded pleased. "Margaret and I found a house we like north of Tampa. It's in a retirement community that isn't too big. Margaret is really excited, and I think I'm going to be happy not to spend another winter here freezing my butt off." He chuckled. "I think my last day working is going to be early October. That way Trevor can find someone to manage the garage in time."

"Sounds great. I'm jealous."

Larry snickered. "Kid, you've got your whole life ahead of you. It's too early to be thinking about retirement. Find yourself someone who will make you as happy as my first wife and now Margaret have made me."

"I'm trying, Larry. I really am."

Brent could almost see Larry rolling his eyes. "So you finally decided to man up and say something to Scott?" He sighed. "Sometimes it takes a real scare before we know what we really want."

"Yeah. But I still wonder if I'm doing the right thing. I am his supervisor and all, and I worry what some of the other guys will think."

Larry laughed. "You know that if it becomes a problem, we'd be more than happy to have Scott and Lee come here to work. Something like that is easily solved. Any of the garages would be thrilled to have them. So worry about what's really important. Like helping that boy get through the hell he has to be enduring." Larry sighed. "After they told me what happened, I tried to understand what he was going through. Margaret is getting hard of hearing and is going to need hearing aids. She's fighting it with everything she has because it makes her feel old. I probably don't hear the way I used to and all, but I think it would be hard not being able to hear at all like that."

"He's doing remarkably well, I think. He's already signed up for sign language classes with his parents, and I have also," Brent said and swallowed hard.

"But you're nervous about it."

"Of course I am. I took Spanish in school and it was a complete disaster. I don't remember a thing and barely passed the class." Languages were most definitely not Brent's strong suit. "And the sites I've been to say that picking up sign language is just as hard as learning any other new language."

"You can do it because you're motivated and have reason to. What good was a teenager going to see in learning Spanish in the middle of Wisconsin? Next to nothing. It was a class to fill your schedule. Taking these classes is going to allow you to talk to someone you care about." Larry had always been one of the most practical guys Brent knew. "Stop second-guessing yourself."

Man, he was much more of an open book than he thought he'd been. "I'll do my best."

"Good. And I'll keep my eyes out for a car like that. I made a few calls to some friends in the area, but I'll call again just in case." Larry rattled off the places so Brent would know. "You realize this is a long shot."

"Fifty to one, but I have to try. The police aren't getting anywhere and it's bothering Scott." Hell, he'd move a mountain if it made Scott happy. "I'm going to get back to work."

"You do that, and I'll let you know if I find out anything." Larry said goodbye and ended the call.

Brent took a few minutes and then began making more phone calls to everyone he knew in the business. He had contacts at various dealerships and phoned them to see if anyone had brought in a car meeting that description with front-end damage.

"We had one," Gary, an acquaintance from the Chevrolet dealership, told him. "That make, model, and color was brought in last week. Let me check on what was done."

"Thanks, Gary. I really appreciate the help." Brent's heart rate picked up as he thought of how lucky he might have gotten.

"No problem...." Gary drew out the last word, attention elsewhere. "Oh. It was for a brake relining and oil change. There wasn't any front-end damage. I'm sorry. Just normal maintenance for a car of that age."

"Okay, Gary. I appreciate it." Brent hung up. He wondered if this was just a waste of time, but shook the thought away. No, he was doing it to help Scott and he'd spend every extra minute he had to do that. Brent sighed and moved down to the next places on his list.

He didn't have any further luck, though. Everyone said they hadn't worked on a car like that in the past few weeks. He wasn't getting anywhere. Maybe the owner just went home and parked the car in the garage until the heat was off. Who the hell knew.

Brent pounded his fist on the top of his desk. He'd wanted to try to do something to help. He had to try. With a sigh he went back to the work he should have been doing. He had plenty, and should have known that he wasn't going to randomly call a garage that just happened to be working on the car that hit Scott.

How is your day so far? Scott texted him that afternoon.

Good. I called a bunch of garages and no one had taken in the car that hit you, but I'm going to keep trying. And Larry says he's going to ask the other managers to keep their eyes open.

Thank you.

Brent put aside the receipts he'd been reviewing. *You're welcome. Have the police said anything more?*

No. Mom and Dad called again this morning, and Dad got mad, yelling at them. At least I got to see him turn completely red, and I thought he might explode.

That was understandable, as far as Brent was concerned. Sometimes the cops needed to be yelled at in order to get them moving. *I'll let you know if I find out anything. What are you doing this afternoon?*

Going crazy sitting on the couch. Mom gave one of her tirades about how I need to heal. I think she's scared for me to go out or something. Brent could almost see Scott going stir-crazy. *I got confirmation of my signing class. It starts in a few weeks.*

Me too, though I don't know if I'm in the same class as you. Tuesday and Thursday nights. Brent sent the text and set his phone on the desk as Clyde passed by the window.

"Lee and I got that car done. He zeroed in on the fuel injectors, and they were partially clogged. We cleaned them out and it's purring like a kitten." Clyde grinned. "What's next?"

"Take a look at the blue Corvette. It needs a full overhaul, and check the brakes. The owner says they're sluggish, so be careful pulling it in."

"Will do." Clyde closed the door, and Brent picked up his phone once again.

That's my class. I asked, and they said it was best if the people I was close to learned at the same time I did. Then we could all practice and learn from each other. Taking the classes will be good, but having someone to practice with is more helpful.

Great. In two weeks some of the communication barriers between them would start to lower. Brent didn't have any illusions that they would go away quickly, but making progress was good.

How late do you have to work?

Until closing. I have things I need to do, and I need the time to get them done. Brent was already tired, but not unhappy about how he'd gotten that way. He and Scott had been up late, and then he had taken Scott home before going on to work.

He knew what Scott was getting at, and his fingers itched to say that he'd be over after work to pick him up, but with the way Carolyn had met him on the porch that morning—her eyes had shot daggers at him—it was probably not a good idea. *How about Wednesday? I can pick you up after work and we can go to dinner.*

You mean eat out?

Sure :)

I haven't done that since the accident. What if someone… I don't know.

It's okay. Brent hated Scott's hesitancy. *We can do whatever you want to do.*

Then, okay. Let's do it. I'll see you Wednesday. :)

Now Brent just needed things to occupy his time until then. He set his phone on the desk and worked, head down, for the rest of the day before dragging himself home and dropping right into bed.

"DARRYL, ARE you done for the day?" Brent asked late Wednesday afternoon.

"What do you need?" Darryl looked up from where he was cleaning his tools. He was old-school. He kept his work area meticulously clean and his tools spotless. It was what he was known for, and woe be it to the guy who borrowed his tools without asking, or worse, without cleaning them afterward.

"Can you stop at Wilson's Body on your way home? They have a part for the Buick Skylark that we need to get it running again. It's the only one I've been able to find in town, and they have it on hold for us." Brent handed Darryl the sheet with the order on it. "They can send us an invoice. Just bring in the part when you come in tomorrow."

"Sure thing." Darryl took the paperwork and put it in his pocket before returning to his task. Once he was done and everything was back where it belonged, he closed and locked his toolbox, left the garage to get into the pristine 1941 Buick that he'd restored to its black beauty perfection, and headed out. His car was the envy of everyone in the garage, including Brent. Every ounce of it was original or repaired with original parts, and he'd won contests with it.

Brent watched him go and then went back to his office, messaging Scott that he'd be there to pick him up in an hour. Then he made sure everything was buttoned down for the night and began the process of locking up. He was done and ready to go on schedule, then made a quick stop at home to shower and change before heading to Scott's to pick him up.

Brent pulled in right on time, and Scott came out to meet him. He opened the door and climbed in. "My mother asked me if I was planning to stay out all night again. She had that pissed-off, disappointed look." He pulled the door closed and sank in his seat. "It's like it's okay for me to be gay, they can handle that, but if I'm actually seeing someone, that's too much for them."

Brent grabbed the pad as a thought hit him. *Or maybe they expect us to behave the way we would if you were straight.*

"Huh?" Scott asked.

If you were their son, going out with girls, they would expect you to behave a certain way and wait for marriage… right? He couldn't believe he was writing this to Scott, but for some weird reason, it made sense to him, given what he knew about Scott's parents. *They want you to be happy, and they want to make sure I'll make you happy. So maybe we invite them over to my house and cook them dinner together? Let them see us working together and that we get along.* He thought that was a pretty good idea, and it would likely help Scott at the same time.

"Okay. As long as you invite your mother too." Scott had an amazing grin, and Brent nodded. His mother would love to meet Scott and his parents. In fact, she'd been asking when that was going to happen. Maybe Scott's folks meeting his mom would let them all see that this was a normal relationship rather than something foreign to what they knew.

Brent pulled away. He hadn't told Scott where they were going. Brent drove toward downtown and got off the freeway heading east. There were a number of restaurants down this way, and Scott seemed a little worried about what Brent had in mind until he pulled up in front of Oakland Gyros, an institution in Milwaukee. Brent's stomach rumbled at the thought of a gyro, fries, and all the sauce he could stand. Dang, this was a home run. And to top it off, he got a parking spot right out front, which had to be some sort of miracle.

Brent got out and waited for Scott before heading inside to wait in line. The place was always busy, even after midnight. He inhaled the heavenly scent of herbs and roasting meat.

"I used to love this place. Mom and Dad used to bring me here. Just get me a gyro platter with fries and a diet soda," Scott said.

Brent nodded and smiled. He placed the order while Scott got a table, then brought the tray over, sat down, and passed out the food and the squeeze bottle of tzatziki. That was the best part. By the end of the meal, he'd have eaten so much garlic that his throat would feel funny, but he didn't care, because every bite was an exercise in Greek-food nirvana.

Scott dug right in, eating like he was starved. "The doctor says I can come back to work next week as long as I promise to take it easy and no heavy lifting."

Brent pulled out his notepad. *That's no problem. All the guys will be so happy to have you back. Lee asks me every day when you're going to come back, and he says he'll bring his computer to make things easier. They all miss you.* That would be another part of Scott's life that could return to normal. Sure, they would need to make accommodations, but that was easy enough to do.

"I miss them too. Even Darryl." Scott smiled. "He's such a fussbudget sometimes, but he's taught me a lot."

Brent laughed. *That's Darryl*, he wrote, then set the pad on the table between them before starting to eat. He squeezed sauce on his gyro meat, grabbed a fork, and took the first amazing bite. There were gyro stands all over town, but this was the best as far as he was concerned, and judging by how quickly Scott tucked in, he thought the same.

After a few minutes, Scott tapped his shoulder and pointed discreetly toward the line at the counter. Marshall, Spencer, and Louie from church were standing there, talking and laughing among themselves. Brent watched closely and saw the moment they noticed Scott, who had paled.

The restaurant was noisy with overlapping conversations, so it was impossible for Brent to hear what they were talking about until they got toward the end of the line. "It's what happens when you ignore God's commandments. He has ways of making sinners pay." Marshall looked toward Scott, and Brent's blood began to boil. He knew he needed to let that shit pass. It was their opinion and they were entitled to it, no matter how ridiculous and small-minded it was.

"Too bad he didn't die," Spencer commented, and Brent had to keep himself from standing and putting these assholes in their place. "Hey, Scotty," Spencer said without turning toward them, "too bad you weren't put out of our misery."

Brent's anger rose further, but there were three of them. He wanted to stand and take them on but did his best to try to ignore them.

Scott took his hand and held it, shaking his head. "Please don't let them bother you. They're assholes, and they can say what they want. At least I don't have to hear it."

Brent turned away to ignore them. Scott was right, and he wasn't up to fighting all of them. Besides, it was a public restaurant.

Do you want to take our food and go? Maybe getting out of there was best.

"Why don't we eat and then we can just leave?" Scott looked around, and Brent did the same, grateful there were no tables open near them. The guys got their food and passed by the table, looking at the two of them before continuing on to a spot near the front windows.

What a great way to ruin the evening. Brent had hoped they could go out and have some fun, maybe have a nice dinner. He so wanted to give Scott a fun evening out. When he turned back to the table, Scott was eating as though nothing had happened. Hell, maybe he was right. Scott couldn't hear it, and maybe he was so immune to their bullshit that he really didn't care. Brent was angry on Scott's behalf, but maybe he was the one ruining the evening.

Brent's phone chimed, and he pulled it out of his pocket. It was a message from Darryl.

I got the parts, and I have something to ask you about in the morning.

Thanks, Brent sent, then put the phone back in his pocket without another thought and returned his attention to where it belonged: on Scott.

"I never liked the phone and now I hate it," Scott said. "People talk on them all the time, and I'm completely cut out."

Brent took his phone back out, opened it, and pressed the Power button, then put it in his pocket with what he hoped was a sexy grin. Scott laughed, a beautiful sound that Brent would never, ever get tired of. Brent glanced over at the holier-than-thous as they glared across the restaurant at Scott, but then he turned away. They weren't important. Their small thoughts and petty actions didn't compare to Scott and his gentleness. Scott was the only person who mattered—not those idiots—and their words couldn't touch him.

Scott finished his dinner and sat back, seemingly happy and contented, and almost instantly the earlier assholeness was forgotten. Brent finished as well, sopping up the last of his sauce with a fry and then standing. He waited for Scott, then protectively placed his hand lightly at the small of his back as they walked toward the exit.

Brent felt three sets of eyes on them as they made their way through the restaurant. Scott had to have felt it too. He stiffened as they reached the door and paused a second before continuing out.

"They're such jerks."

Brent nodded but didn't reach for the pad in his pocket. Instead he curled his fingers into a fist. By the time they were in the car, his anger had dissipated, replaced with shame. God, those guys had been making fun of and picking on Scott, and he'd done nothing. He'd sat at the table and wished they'd go away. He hadn't stood up for him or anything. Rather, that damn coward gene had taken over again. Heat rose in his cheeks, and Brent gripped the wheel so tightly, his knuckles hurt. He let go, fumbled with the keys to get them in the ignition, and then started the car and cranked the air-conditioning to quickly cool the interior.

"I really hate those guys. They completely miss the point," Scott said.

Brent turned and shrugged, then drove out of the lot. He wasn't sure what Scott was getting at, but he didn't want to grab a pad and ask. More than anything Brent wanted to get out of here.

"The whole thing with religion is to be good to your neighbor. Treat your brother as yourself. They all think if they do the right things, feel the right way, say the right stuff, then they're doing what the church wants. But that isn't right. Their actions don't match how they feel. They're small, petty guys. Especially Spencer, who is living a lie and willing to make himself and the people around him miserable to defend it." Scott sighed as Brent made the turn to take them back toward home.

He couldn't argue with Scott right now, and wished he didn't feel the way he did. But, damn it all, he hated feeling like a coward all the fucking time. He was strong enough. Hell, he wasn't a skinny kid any longer. Brent had gone to the gym for years, lifting weights to get bigger. But that didn't seem to matter. He was still that scared little boy hiding and running away when danger or a threat made an appearance.

"Stop it," Scott snapped, and Brent pulled to a halt at the light. "I can see those thoughts churning in your head. Making a scene in the restaurant wouldn't have helped anyone, and it only would have gotten us kicked out. They would have looked high and mighty, and you would have looked bad."

In his heart Brent knew Scott was right, but it didn't counter the sinking, wormy feeling in his belly. He hadn't stood up for Scott with those bullies, and he damn well should have. The voice in his head berated him the entire way home. Once he parked, they went up to his apartment and Brent turned on the television, making sure the closed captioning showed. He just wanted to sit, watch something stupid, and try to forget all about those assholes.

Brent pulled out his phone and turned it back on to check for any messages. There was a text from Darryl asking what kind of car had hit Scott's. Brent sent the information, put the phone on silent, and tossed it onto the coffee table.

"You need to stop letting them bother you."

Brent snatched a pad off the table. *But they were being cruel to you, and I didn't do anything about it.*

Scott sat back, laughing. "I know what they were saying, and I don't really care anymore. They're jerks, and I don't need to listen to them. Besides, I don't need you to fight my battles for me. If I need to take them on, I can do that. They're a bunch of blowhard asses who are all talk. Yeah, I don't want to be around them, and the way I figure it, a church they belong to is a place I don't want to be." Scott took his hand. "I'm happy to have you as my boyfriend. You don't need to take on the role of knight in shining armor as well."

But dammit, Brent wanted to be his knight—he wanted to fight for Scott. Hell, he kept thinking he'd go to battle for him and do whatever was necessary to support and help him, yet when the time came, he folded like a house of cards. Brent sighed and sat back, closing his eyes and wishing he could disappear.

Scott took his hand, threading his fingers through them. "Just let it go."

Brent wished he could. But the underlying shame he'd carried for a long time wasn't just going to go away, no matter how much he wanted it to. Brent nodded because it was easier than trying to explain everything to Scott. He wasn't ready to talk about it with anyone. Brent had shared some things with Scott about his dad, and that was more than he'd done with anyone other than his mother. Trevor and Dean didn't even know about that part of his life, which indicated how deeply he'd kept it buried all these years.

"You can't, can you?" Scott said, turning toward him. "You may nod and tell me you will, but you won't… you can't." His gaze pierced deeply, and Brent wanted to squirm, anything to make it stop. "I can see you, who you really are… sometimes."

Scott handed him a pad, pressing it into his hand. Then he crossed his arms over his chest, gaze hard, waiting.

I wish I could, Brent wrote. *I'll be okay.* He breathed deeply to try to clear his head. He had more important things in mind than letting a group of assholes ruin their evening together. *Were those guys always like that?*

Scott shook his head. "They used to be pretty fun. When we were young kids, we were in the same Sunday school classes, and the five of us were holy terrors. Get us in the same room and trouble was going to erupt. At one point they figured I was smarter, so they moved me up to a higher class to separate some of us. It didn't really work too well." Scott sighed. He was speaking a little loudly, but Brent said nothing about it. Volume was going to be an issue for Scott unless he decided to speak really softly all the time, and there was no use in that. Scott needed to be heard the same as everyone else. He deserved that.

"I guess we grew older. Spencer's dad is a deacon, and Marshall's father is on a number of committees and his mother was the music director. So they were involved and weren't going to be embarrassed by their sons. They closed ranks when things got bad in youth group, and I was labeled a troublemaker. My parents stuck up for me, but even so, I had to meet with the priest on a weekly basis." Scott rolled his eyes. "That was really helpful. Father Closet Case trying to council me on what it meant to be a good Christian man. He actually tried to push me toward the priesthood. Can you imagine?"

Brent stared at him for a moment, then wrote and handed Scott the note. *That must have been terrible. With everyone pushing you in one direction or another.*

"It was. But I was strong and told them all to go to hell. I remember telling the priest that I knew my own mind and I certainly didn't need him to tell me what was right and wrong." Scott snickered. "It was on the edge of my tongue to call him out, but I didn't. I also never went back to youth group and only attended mass with my parents after that. Just like last Sunday… and only when they made me." Scott wiped his eyes. "I was set to move out in a couple of months. But with the accident and then being deaf, I'm not sure when I'll be able to do that."

You can live on your own.

Scott shook his head. "I may be able to eventually, but right now I need too much support. I don't know what others are saying. What they want. Most people are blank to me. Once I learn to read lips and understand the other tools that I need to get along, I think I can." He leaned closer, and Brent held him as he cried softly.

Brent had known this was coming. Scott had to work through what he'd lost, the same way that Brent had grieved for his dad. A part of himself was gone—that was how Brent understood it—and Scott had to accept it and let go so he could move forward and develop the skills he needed to function as a deaf man. Brent wanted to help, but there was only so much he could do. Mostly it was up to Scott, with the rest of the people in his life there to try to support him. That was a heavy weight to bear for anyone.

"Do you know what I thought?" Scott whispered, his voice rough. "I realized I couldn't hear, and then I wondered how anyone was going to love me."

Brent caressed his arm gently, letting Scott know he was there. This wasn't the time for notes and things like that.

"Then I saw you. Right there, and you looked at me like I was precious and special." Scott held him tight, resting his head on Brent's shoulder. "I keep wondering when that look is going to fade, but I see it all the time. You do a lot for me, but I keep wondering what I can do for you. I keep coming up empty. There isn't anything that you need from me." Scott backed away, his eyes filled with moisture. "I worry it's always going to be that way. I'm going to be a burden to everyone in my life, and I don't want that." He gulped and then coughed hard.

Brent had to get a pad. *You do realize that you'll never be a burden because you don't want to be.* Brent gently cupped the back of Scott's head as he read.

"How do you know all this stuff?"

Brent chuckled and reluctantly pulled his hands away to write as quickly as he could to get his thoughts out. *I was unemployed for three months, and I ended up watching a lot of awful daytime television, and that was one of the things I picked up, I guess. I believe we have a lot to do with how well our lives go.*

"That's bullshit!" Scott spat.

Is it? Brent wrote.

"I didn't ask to be deaf, and I certainly didn't hit the back of my own car." Scott was angry, voice raised.

Brent waved a hand and wrote again, then turned the page so Scott could see it. *No, you didn't. But life throws shit at us, and how we handle it says a lot about who we are and the kind of life we're going to lead.* He wanted to crawl under the sofa. He was such a hypocrite sometimes. How could he possibly say stuff like this to Scott when he didn't take that same advice?

"Then why is life throwing everything it has at me? Maybe it could pay attention to someone else for a while." Scott forced a smile, but it faded quickly. "I know what I'm going to do, and I'm not going to let the deafness or anything else win. But it sure would be nice if something good happened. I could certainly use it."

Brent stared at him. He liked to think that maybe he was that something good.

"You know what I mean." Scott hugged him again, and Brent felt better. "You have been the bright spot in all of this."

Brent settled back against the cushions, tossing the pad on the coffee table. He figured he'd given out enough clichéd advice for one night. He really hadn't expected to be having this kind of conversation tonight. But if it was what Scott needed, that was fine.

"Can we talk about something fun?"

Brent nodded vigorously.

"Do you like to do things in winter?" Scott asked. "I love to go skiing. My dad and I used to go a few times each winter. Dad and Mom would rent a cabin at one of the resorts up north. Mom would sit in the lodge near the fire and talk to people while Dad and I hit the slopes." He made schussing motions with his hands. "I'm pretty good too—at least I was."

"You can still ski." Brent made hand motions to go with his words, and Scott understood.

"I know, but it won't be the same. What about you? Do you ski?"

Brent nodded. "I'm very good." He reached for the damn pad again. *So is my mom. She and I used to go. Mom was a real snow bunny when she was young. We have pictures of her. I also like snowmobiling. It's fun zooming over the snow.*

"Me too. Dad has one in the garage, so when we get snow, it's a blast. He has a trailer too, and we'd take it when we went north. There are lots of trails up there. Maybe we could go this winter."

Trevor and James would probably love it too. James is a real speed demon, at least according to Trevor. I doubt he'd go skiing, but we'd all have fun. It was hot as all hell outside and felt like the heat was building in to stay for a while, so it was nice to talk about something cool.

"Maybe we could all go?" Scott said. "It would be nice to plan something and have a trip to look forward to. Everything is so immediate right now. I had a lot of plans about getting an apartment, maybe with Lee. I was going to try to get a new car. I wanted to travel a little. My mom would freak, but I wanted to get a motorcycle like Trevor's and travel around the country. All that is different now."

It doesn't have to be, Brent wrote.

Scott grabbed the pad and put it behind his back. "Right. Without the fucking pad, you can't talk to me. No one can. It's the only way anyone has to communicate with me, and it's not going to change a whole hell of a lot. If I'm alone, I have to wear a fucking sign that says I'm deaf so please have pity on me and write down what you want to say. Even when I learn to sign, I'll only be able to use it with people who can sign. If you want to be part of my life, be prepared to spend it translating for me." Scott rolled his eyes. "That sucks, Brent. It really does. I don't want that for you, and I don't want to have to wait to learn what anyone is saying."

Brent reached for the pad, but Scott pushed it farther away. He tried to get it, but Scott sat in his way, so Brent reached around him and ran his hands over his side.

"That's not fair!" Scott cried, through peals of laughter. "I'm going to be sore." Brent pulled back, making tickling motions, and Scott handed him the pad. "You're mean."

"I am not." He leaned forward to capture Scott's lips. He'd been doing a lot of talking lately, and Brent was starting to think he could put those sweet lips to another use. Scott didn't seem to mind as he wound his arms around Brent's neck. He held Scott closer and forgot about his worries and what happened at the restaurant.

"You can make me forget my own name most of the time," Scott told him.

Brent didn't respond but thought, *Mission accomplished.* He smiled, cupping Scott's cheeks in his hands, guiding him into another kiss. Brent would have loved to stay just like this forever, sucking lightly on Scott's lower lip, listening to the soft, involuntary sounds he made. Brent was willing to bet that Scott had no idea he was making them, and that made it all the more thrilling. It told Brent just how happy and excited he was making Scott. That thought sent his own excitement through the roof, and he had to restrain himself from pressing Scott back into the sofa, stripping him down, and tasting him all over. His willpower wavered as their kiss deepened, Brent slipping his hand under Scott's shirt, the smooth, hot skin and muscles rippling under it. Damn, Scott was beautiful, and Brent didn't need to see him to know that. He could feel it as he stroked upward and his thumb located a pert nipple, teasing it as Scott quivered under him. There was nothing in this world more exciting to Brent than a man shaking in unbridled passion.

"You're stunning," Brent said. "I know you can't hear me, but you make me want you." He reached for Scott's belt and unfastened it as Scott gulped and stilled.

Brent's phone vibrated, and he stilled as well. He was coming to hate that thing. Brent knew he should have left the damn thing off, but now it vibrated like hell on the wooden top.

Scott turned toward where Brent was looking, and the excitement left him in an instant. "You should get that." He sat up as Brent reached for the phone, then stared out the window as Brent answered it.

"Brent, it's Darryl. I'm sorry to bother you, but the more I thought about it, the more I realized I needed to talk to you. I was at Wilson's today."

"Yeah, I know." Brent tried not to be short with him. Whatever was bothering Darryl had him in a tizzy, and Darryl was never like that. Methodical and patient, not jittery and uptight. "What's going on?"

"Well, I know you were calling around and put the word out about the car that hit Scott. Did you call Wilson's and ask them if they had a car like that?" Darryl asked tentatively.

"Of course." Brent rolled his eyes. "They were one of the first places I called after Trevor's other garages. Why?"

"Because when I was there, I looked into the service garage and saw a red Malibu about the right year. It was in one of the bays and looked like it was being taken apart to start repair. It had definitely been in a front-end collision. I don't know when it came in or anything, but I thought you would want to know."

Brent blinked a few times to try to take this in. "Thanks. But how did you know I was making calls?"

"Lee heard you." Darryl paused. "You made the kid cry with what you're doing to help Scott. So when I went… I wasn't looking or expecting to see the car. I was just seeing what they were working on and…."

"I understand that. Professional curiosity." Brent sat on the edge of the sofa, his body filling with tension by the second. He had called Wilson's, and the serviceman who answered the phone had said they hadn't had a car like that. "What's your impression of when the car came in?"

"I've known Brian Gunderson for a long time, and he said it's been sitting in the back for a week or more. I tried not to make a big deal about it, but if they said they didn't have that kind of car, someone lied. And I like Scott, and he deserves to find out who did this to him." The anger coming through Darryl's voice was palpable. "Brain said they had been holding it in the back, waiting for the owner to make a decision on the repairs. He said the guy wasn't insured or wasn't going through his insurance. I was going to tell you in the morning, but thought that it might be better to call you tonight."

Brent nodded to himself, his heart racing a mile a second. Scott turned, and Brent smiled brightly at him, taking his hand as Darryl continued talking.

"That son of a bitch lied to me," Brent growled, seconds later, wishing he'd taken down the name of the guy he'd spoken with. Brent tried to clear his head and think. He'd written a bunch of useless stuff while he'd been on the phone, but there was no way to discern if he'd…. "Shit…." Brent groaned. "I talked to Howard when I called."

"Grinnel is a weasel," Darryl commented, and Brent wished he could argue with him. He should have been more careful about who he'd talked to, but the thought of someone lying to him hadn't crossed his mind. "I used to work with him when I was at Ashendorf's, and he was a slimy bastard then. What do you want me to do?"

"Right now, nothing. Don't tell anyone else what you saw. I need some time to think and to talk with Scott. We don't even know if this is the car that hit him, but it seems strange that they would lie to me about it unless they had something to hide." Brent's head ached. "I wish to fuck I could get a look at that car."

Darryl was silent for a few heartbeats. "Maybe you can."

"How?" Brent asked right away.

"Like I said, Gunderson is a good friend. His wife and my wife are in the same garden club, and we took a vacation together a few years ago. I can ask him if he can let us in the garage to take a look at it. Let me make a call and I'll get back to you."

"Thanks." Brent hung up and turned to Scott, who was chewing on his lower lip. He tapped him on the shoulder.

"What's going on?" Scott was so nervous, he seemed like he was going to fly apart. "I can feel something is wrong."

Brent shifted closer to him and reached for the pad, then hesitated before he started to write. Scott read the note over his shoulder, growing paler by the second. *That was Darryl. I had asked him to get some parts from Wilson's today. He says he saw a Malibu, red, between the years the police told us, in one of the bays. I had called them and they lied to me about it.*

"Should we call the police?"

Brent shrugged and then wrote. *We don't know if this is the car. But the bastards lied to me, so someone has something to hide.* His phone rang, and he snatched it up. "Yeah, Darryl?"

"Brian has a key and says he'll meet you there. It seems he's been wondering what Howard is up to. Anyway, he'll meet you there in half an hour."

"Thanks. Tell him I'll be there." Brent had to know if this was the car, and this seemed like the best way to do it. After that, he could call the police and they could take it from there. Brent hung up and explained what was happening, as best he could, to Scott.

"I'm going with you," Scott said.

Brent shook his head, adamant. "No!"

"I am going." Scott crossed his arms over his chest. "If this is the car that hit me, I want to see it. I need to." The unmistakable pain and steel in his voice made Brent waver.

Brent grabbed the notepad. *I don't want you in any danger*. God, the thought of anything happening to Scott had Brent's stomach roiling.

"We're going to a garage to look at a car. Nothing more. No one else is going to be there." Scott leaned forward. "I'm not helpless." The last was said as a challenge.

Brent closed his eyes and nodded once. It was all he could do. He didn't care that they were only going to a garage to look at a car. This could be the car that had hit him, and it could very well lead them to the person who had hurt Scott. But Brent's belly clenched as he thought of Scott going along. Yet he couldn't realistically tell him no. Scott had the right to make his own decisions.

"Then when do we go?"

"Now." Brent stood and got his keys. He waited for Scott, and they left the apartment. Brent locked the door and they walked down to his car.

The drive to Wilson's didn't take very long, and there was a single car with a light on inside parked next to the main door. Brent pulled up next to it and they got out to meet Brian.

"Thank you for doing this."

Brian nodded. "I figured it was either you or the police. If you truly believe this is the car you're looking for, then you do what you need to. I'm only trying to prevent unwanted attention to the business."

"Of course." Brent turned to Scott and made introductions. "Can we see it?"

Brian unlocked the door and they went inside, through the reception and waiting area, to the shop floor. He followed Brian as they approached a red Malibu. The car's front end was a mess. It had been in a severe accident and seemed barely driveable. There were scrapes and pieces of paint on it. Brent stepped closer, pulling out his phone to use it as a light for a closer look.

"There are dark blue paint scrapes." The color of Scott's car. "Have you started work?"

"Howard got it brought in, and it's his job to complete the work. I think he's ordered parts." Brian motioned and took him off to the side. "This is the scrap room, and there's what he's removed so far."

Brent checked out the parts and turned to Scott, who leaned against the doorframe, holding it to stay upright.

"This is it," Scott breathed, and Brent had to agree. It was likely.

"I need to call the police."

"I will," Brian offered. "I'll do it after you leave, on suspicion that a car we are working on has been party to an accident that we don't think has been reported. I'll just say I was working late. It's no problem. Howard said that it was his cousin's car and that it had been hit a while ago."

Brent turned to Scott, pulled out the pad from his pocket, and wrote him a quick note to explain.

"Can you get the name?" Brent asked, and Brian pulled a scrap of paper from his pocket and handed it to him. Brent shoved it in his pocket, jotted down the license plate details, and they left the service area. "I appreciate the help. You have to call this in, or I will, and that won't be good."

"Nope. I'll call it in. That way we're cooperating with the police." Brian groaned. "So help me, if that ass Howard has brought some of his shit here, I'm going to kill him and then turn him over to my uncle so he can bring him back and kill the shithead again."

"Your uncle?"

"Yeah." Brian sighed. "Old man Wilson is my uncle. He wants me to take over for him eventually, but with this kind of trouble showing up, there isn't going to be shit-all to take over. I told Uncle Rob to can Howard, but my uncle is loyal to his people. Now look what that got him."

"I understand, and we don't want to cause any trouble for you, only the guy who hit Scott and anyone who tried to cover it up." Hell, Brent was so angry, he could hardly see straight.

"You better go, and I'll make that call." Brian already had his phone out, so Brent and Scott headed to the main entrance. Brent listened as Brian talked to the police. The night was relatively quiet, with only a few cars passing by. He and Scott got into his car, and Brent turned to Scott once the door was closed.

Scott was shaking, head down. "That was the car that hit me."

Brent nodded and took Scott's hand. He needed to know he was going to be all right. "I think so." He grabbed the pad from his pocket. *There's nothing to fear here. It's just a car. It can't hurt you now.* He had a likely name in his pocket, but he didn't want to show it to Scott. Not yet, because there was the possibility that this wasn't the car. The police would need to figure that out.

"Okay." Scott sank into the seat, and Brent pulled out of the parking area. He headed for Scott's parents' house, thinking it was probably best if he took him home. Plus they needed to know what was going on.

"We aren't going back to your apartment?" Scott watched out the side window and didn't seem angry enough to challenge him, so he took Scott home, pulling into the drive.

Carolyn rushed out of the house, and Scott got out of the car. Brent hurried around and walked with him up to the front door, where Scott fell into her arms. "Brent found the car, Mom." Scott held her, and Brent wished it was him Scott was clinging to. "He and one of the guys at work."

She looked over Scott's shoulder. "Are you sure?"

"Fairly. The police have been called. One of the garage managers is doing that as we speak. I also have the license number and the name of the owner. I haven't told Scott yet, because I thought it best that I bring him home."

"But he saw the car?"

Brent nodded and followed them inside, closing the door behind him. Scott settled on the sofa, and Brent filled Carolyn and Reggie in on what they'd found. He sat next to Scott, holding his hand, Scott clutching his in return. Brent would do anything to make this pain go away for Scott. Hell, he'd take it on a dozen times over if it meant seeing one of Scott's smiles.

"If it's the car, they'll find out who owns it, and that should lead them to who hit Scott," Reggie said, gently holding Carolyn's hand.

"Well." Brent reached into his pocket to hold the slip of paper in his fist. "My friend gave me the name of the owner. But I don't know what we should do with it until we know if it's the car." He held his breath. If Scott or his folks asked for it, he'd give it to them, but he hoped they didn't. Not yet.

Reggie shook his head. "I don't want to know. If it's someone I've heard of or an acquaintance, I'd be tempted to go over and tear their lungs out." He pounded the arm of his chair. "It's best if I don't even know. Does he?"

"No." Brent leaned into Scott, and then all of them caught Scott up on the conversation they'd been having. Brent admitted to having the name, but Scott pulled back, not wanting to know either.

"I'll let the police tell me. Then I'll know for sure." Scott stood and hugged both his parents before kissing Brent good night.

Brent left the house and drove home to his complex. Once he got there, Brent went up to his place and inside. Then, and only then, did he hazard a peek at the name on the paper.

CHAPTER 6

THREE DAYS of waiting and hoping....

His dad called the police and talked to the officer in charge of the investigation. They had gotten the call about the car and had been down to check into it. Samples of the paint from the car had been taken, and they were waiting for tests to prove it was the one that hit him. That's all they told them, and Scott was on pins and needles.

He checked his watch and went to the front window to look for Brent. It was Saturday afternoon and Scott was going to go to the garage for the rest of the day. He was hoping to be able to get to work a little and learn his way around the garage once again.

Brent pulled into the drive, and Scott said goodbye to his mother and rushed out to the car.

"Do you think this is going to be weird, you know, because of us?" Scott asked as he fastened his seat belt.

Brent simply shook his head as he backed out of the drive. The times when they were in the car were some of the hardest. Conversations were one-way. Scott could talk, but Brent couldn't communicate much in return. His hands were busy, so yes and no answers were about the limit.

"It... will... be... fine...," Brent said to him slowly.

"I suppose. You have your work to do, and so will I." Scott shared a smile with Brent, excited to be doing something normal, even for a few hours. He hoped that he could go back to work full-time the following week, but he had to figure out how he was going to make that happen. He had energy and the soreness was largely gone. It was time. But he was nervous too. What if he wasn't able to do his job any longer? That thought was always in the back of his mind. Scott knew he could figure out ways to help the guys communicate with him, but what about customers? "I need to relax and stop thinking about all this stuff in my head over and over."

Brent patted his leg gently. He pulled to a stop and opened the console between the seats to hand Scott a pad. He was surprised to see a letter.

> *Scott,*
> *You will be just fine today because you're strong and you love what you do. I have no doubt that you can do anything you set your mind to. You're smart and a brilliant mechanic. Take the time to get your feet under you and don't be afraid to ask for help. Deaf people are scientists, nurses, engineers, and just about anything else you can think of, so you can be deaf and be a great mechanic. I have faith in you, and so does Trevor, as well as the rest of your colleagues. They are all looking forward to your return. So when things get difficult or frustrating, just ask for help.*
> *We are all there for you.*
> *Brent.*

Damn. Brent had known he wasn't able to talk to him while they rode, so he'd put his thoughts in a note. Scott read it again and then removed the page from the notebook, folded it, and put it in his pocket. "Thank you." If Brent had said those words to him, Scott would have thought they were nice. What surprised him was that seeing them written down and being able to read them over again made it more solid.

He let Brent drive in peace and watched as the buildings passed by. The closer they got to work, the more excited Scott grew. They turned into the lot, and Brent pulled into his usual spot. Scott practically jumped out of the car and hurried inside. He inhaled deeply, the scent of grease and oil familiar and strangely comforting. It meant he was home in a way, at a place where he was useful and could contribute.

Clyde brought Lee over, and Lee hugged Scott tight. It felt so good to be with his friend again.

"I'm doing okay," Scott told him. As usual, communication was one-way, but he led Lee back to their spot. Lee made his way over to where he'd been working and returned with his tablet, which he set up near their toolboxes.

I missed you, Lee typed. *Just so you know, you aren't allowed to do that again. You scared the crap out of me. I thought I was going to lose my best friend.*

"I promise I'll do my best." Scott knew Lee had been worried and his teasing was just a way of letting that out. "So what are you working on?"

Clyde and I just finished a brake job. So now I'm free to work with you again. Brent told me he has another relining for us to do. Clyde is going to bring it in for us, and we can get started. Lee vibrated with excitement as he typed.

"Great. I'm dressed and ready, so we can get to work." Scott touched Lee's arm. "I really am doing well, and I think they might have found the car that hit me, so it's just a matter of time before they find the guy."

Clyde said they were hopeful that your hearing might come back. Has it at all? Lee typed.

"No. I thought it might for a while, but it isn't. A few times I thought I might be hearing things, but it was in my head. They were just phantom sounds of some type."

I had those too, with my sight. I used to see flashes sometimes and thought I was getting my vision back, but it was the same sort of thing. I'd stand in the sun and feel the warmth and then I'd think I could see light, but it was just my body associating the warmth of the sun with the light. Lee smiled sadly at him. *I'm really sorry this is happening to you.*

"It's okay. I'm taking it one day at a time and figuring things out." Scott hugged Lee once again. "Do you want to get started?"

After Clyde brought in the car, they got into position and slowly began removing the wheels to get to the brakes. Things went as well as Scott could have hoped. The job took longer than usual because they needed to develop ways to communicate with each other. A lot more of what they did together was through touch, but in the end, the brake pads were changed and the repair completed. Clyde checked their work for them, and they were good to go.

Scott took a brief break to get a drink and a breath of fresh air. As he stepped outside, a car pulled into the lot. As soon as Scott saw the driver, he groaned and went back inside. "We have an unwelcome customer," Scott told Brent, and he stood, glancing out of the window.

"I got it," Brent said, and Scott knew he should go back to work, but he was dying to know why Spencer would be here. He left the office as Spencer entered the work area and approached when he saw Scott, his mouth moving a mile a minute.

"You do realize I'm deaf," Scott told him, rolling his eyes. "That means I can't hear you." He reached to the desk and handed him a pad and pen, then waited while Spencer wrote his note.

I need to talk to you. I asked around and found out where you worked. His hand shook, and Scott wondered what they could possibly have to talk about.

"If you need work on your car, you can talk to my boss, and he'll see if we have any room on the schedule. Other than that, I don't think there's much to say to each other." Scott looked around. "I know what you want to believe happened all those years ago, and you and your friends have made my life miserable

ever since. Now you want something… Lord knows what….”
This was the weirdest visit Scott had ever had in his life.

Spencer shifted from foot to foot as Brent came over. He
talked to Spencer, who looked around, confused, and then Brent
escorted him back to his car and watched until Spencer was gone
before returning to Scott.

What did he want?

Scott shrugged. “I have no idea. He said we needed to talk,
but I didn’t have anything to say, and I was going to ask him to
leave.” He turned to where Spencer had gone. “I don’t know
what he wants.”

Brent heaved a deep breath and motioned toward the office.
Scott followed him, and Brent closed the door after them. Then
he pulled out his wallet and withdrew a small piece of paper.

“Is that the name from the other night?” Scott asked, and
Brent nodded, handing the piece of paper to him. Scott opened it
and paled, looking up at Brent to make sure this was real. “He’s
the asshole who hit me?”

Brent reached for the pad on his desk. *I don’t know for sure,
but he owns the car that we saw at the garage, and now he was
here to see you. I expect he was trying to scope things out and
see if you knew anything. I mean, if you went ballistic when he
showed up, he’d know that you knew he’d hit you.*

“What did you tell him?”

*That you were busy and had work to do. If he wanted to
talk to you, then he needed to do it on his own time. That guy
is creepy. He kept looking around at everyone except me.* Brent
shivered, and Scott was seconds from doing the same.

Scott turned away, trying to get a handle around the fact
that one of the holier-than-thous had actually hit him. His hands
clenched to fists. “What a fucking asshole. He looks down on me
for who I am, but that bastard hits me, sends me to the hospital,
does all this stuff to me, and then drives away and expects that
he’s going to get away with it.”

Brent wrote frantically. *He isn't. The police are handling it, and you need to stay away from him.*

"Do my parents know?" Scott asked but found it hard to talk around the anger and huge lump of bile that kept rising in his throat.

Brent shook his head. *Your dad didn't want to know. He was afraid if he did, he'd do something he'd regret.* He tossed the pad aside and pulled Scott into a hug.

Scott had no idea what the hell he was going to do. His world had just been turned on its head again. The accident had been bad enough, and thinking about some nameless, faceless person hitting him and driving away was one thing. But someone he knew and had once been friends with?

"Why would someone do this to me?" Scott asked, his throat rough and scratchy. "What the hell did I ever do to him that was so bad that he would do this? I know he thinks I'm a threat to his illusion of straightness, but what the fucking hell?" He clung to Brent because if he didn't, he was going to scream and go running through the garage, throwing everything he could get his damn hands on.

Scott closed his eyes and tried to calm the roiling, churning pit of despair and acrimony that whirled in his gut. After a few seconds, he began picturing Spencer laid out on the road with cars rolling over him until he was as flat as a pancake, like in an old Bugs Bunny cartoon. *Hell, that's too fucking good for him.* "They should string him up by his toes, or worse, they should make him deaf so he can know what he did to me." Scott shook like a leaf, as wave after wave of meanness and cruelty washed over him. "Spencer needs to fucking suffer."

More than anything right now, he wished he could hear Brent, just once. He needed a soothing voice to help calm him down and stop the parade of mayhem and destruction going through his head.

Brent stroked his back slowly, up and down, and the anger dissipated, leaving Scott confused and as agitated as he'd ever been.

"I have to go back to work," Scott said, needing to do something to get this out of his mind.

Brent released him and grabbed the pad off the desk. *Are you sure you're going to be okay?*

"Somehow."

I wasn't going to show you the name because we don't know for sure. There's a possibility that the car isn't the one that hit you.

Scott shrugged. He knew in his heart that was the car. He'd felt it that night, and he was even more certain now. The only thing still nagging at the back of his mind was whether Spencer had known it was him and left him there. Did Spencer hit him on purpose? That question sent a chill up his spine that nearly buckled his legs. Sure, he and Spencer didn't care for each other, but Scott didn't want to think Spencer would want to hurt him that way… on purpose.

I think hitting your car was an accident, Brent wrote.

"How did you know I was wondering that?" Scott asked.

Because I'd wonder the same thing in your position. I think he was scared shitless and took off without thinking about it. He probably had a lot to drink and wasn't thinking clearly. When he hit you, the only thing he could think about was getting the hell out of there. Brent slipped the pad in his pocket before pulling out his phone. He brought up Scott's home number and showed him the display.

Scott shook his head. He didn't want Brent to call his parents. He needed to figure out how to deal with this on his own, and he wasn't going to run home to Mommy and Daddy at the first moment. "I'll be okay." He breathed deeply, and Brent hugged him again. Scott closed his eyes, inhaling Brent's scent, letting it calm him. In his arms, Scott was safe. Nothing was going to happen to him while Brent was close.

Scott stepped back and gave Brent's hand a quick squeeze before leaving the office.

Lee was waiting for him, and they got busy on the next job. Scott found it hard to concentrate at first, but Lee was counting on him to be his eyes, just like Scott needed Lee to be his ears, so he had to be on his game, and dammit, whatever had happened the night of the accident, it was going to come out in the end. Scott would have to make sure it did. There were too many questions he needed the answers to.

SCOTT MADE it through the end of the day without too many issues. Communicating with Lee was still extra work, but Scott had missed his friend so much, and it was nice to be working with him again. Things weren't the same, though, just like they weren't with anyone else in his life.

Are you doing okay? The day wasn't too much for you, was it? Brent wrote after Scott sat down on the sofa in Brent's apartment. He was tired and satisfied. He had made it through the long afternoon, and now the garage was closed and they were alone. The rest of the world, complete with assholes who drove away from accidents, was outside the door. Scott was doing his best to put them out of his mind. He'd have to deal with the facts soon enough. Stressing wasn't going to do him any good until he knew for sure, and then he'd rip Spencer apart.

"No. The work part was fine. The rest of it was hard."

What do you want to do? The police have the car and are just waiting for the tests. If they come back positive, then they can take him in and question him. If he did hit you and then drove away, he'll be in huge trouble. Brent sat down next to him, letting him read the note. *We can't give away that we know.*

"But he's going to know. His cousin works at Wilson's, and I'm sure he'll have told him that the police were interested in his car. He's already shown up here at work. What if he causes trouble at home?" Scott shook a little. "I mean, what kind of sane, stable person just drives away from an accident when someone has been hurt like I was?" In his effort to figure this whole thing out, Scott only ended up going in circles.

Do you want to forget all about this for a while? Brent wrote, and when Scott nodded, Brent tossed the pad aside, stood, and helped Scott to his feet. Then he slowly led him out of the room, turning out the lights.

In the bedroom Scott stood in the center with Brent behind him. Strong arms wound around his chest. It was pitch-dark, and that was fine. Scott didn't want to see; he only wanted to feel.

Brent's searing hands slid under his shirt, pushed the fabric upward, then plucked his nipples, sending sheer delight running through him. Brent didn't seem to be in any hurry. When Scott lifted his arms, Brent tugged his shirt off over his head and drew him closer. Heated lips skimmed along his shoulders as a huge, strong hand cupped his pec, teasing his nipple until Scott's knees threatened to buckle under him. Still Brent didn't stop. He sucked lightly at the base of Scott's neck, hot breath smoothing over his skin.

"That's really nice." Scott leaned back against Brent's solid form. So much in his life that he'd counted on was turning to quicksand under his feet. At least it felt that way sometimes. Work and even everyday things he'd taken for granted were no longer there, or were so much harder than they were just a month or so ago.

Scott let his arms dangle, releasing his worries while Brent lightly stroked down his chest and side. The scars were healed now, just sensitive, and Brent avoided them for the most part. "It's nice to be touched."

Brent held him a little tighter, sucking at the base of his neck, stroking long and slow over Scott's chest and down his quivering belly. Scott held his breath as Brent teased above his belt, willing Brent to go farther and shifting to give him access should he slide his hand down into his jeans. But Brent didn't. He stepped back and guided Scott to sit on the side of the bed and then lie back. Brent lay next to him.

Hot breath ghosted over Scott's belly, followed by molten lips and a tongue that blazed a trail upward until those lips curled around his nipple. Scott moaned softly, the air rumbling through his chest. He couldn't hear it, but he could feel it, and Brent shook next to him.

Brent's lips danced over Scott's chest and then down his belly, his fingers opening Scott's belt and then the button at the top of his jeans. Brent popped the rest until his jeans spread open. It was sublime, and Scott lay back, unmoving, letting Brent have full control. It felt good to be taken care of, petted, even adored. Brent kissed him as he ran a hand over his chest and belly without stopping, sliding the waistband of his briefs down. His fingers slid over Scott's cock, and waves of desire overtook him when Brent gripped him.

"I wish I knew what you were saying to me." Scott placed his fingers at Brent's neck. The vibrations of his words tickled his fingertips, but he had no idea what Brent was telling him. Brent just kissed him harder, pushed him onto the soft mattress, and he shifted around him until Brent pressed his chest to Scott's before sliding down him, taking the last of Scott's clothes as he went.

Opening his eyes, Scott blinked as the sensation and heat slipped away. There was just enough light for him to see Brent taking off his clothes. Then a naked and beautifully excited Brent climbed back onto the bed and waited as Scott got comfortable. Brent straddled him, their bodies connected, lips to lips, chest to chest, legs sliding along each other, cocks throbbing slightly as Brent moved his hips in delicious time to Scott's ever-faster beating heart. He held Brent, taking in the muscles of his back as he explored downward to cup Brent's firm asscheeks.

"Damn, you feel good." He smiled as Brent smiled back at him.

"So do you," Brent answered simply, pointing at him, then nipped at his lower lip.

Scott arched under him, wanting more, but as Brent reached to the nightstand, Scott held still. The glint of foil caught the sliver of light from between the curtains. He thought Brent dropped it on the bed, but didn't really care because Brent gripped him tighter, kissing harder, his fingers dipping lower, sending little, thrilling ripples of anticipation racing from head to toe.

Slick fingers teased him, and Scott parted his legs farther, needing to give what Brent wanted, getting everything in return. The lingering soreness in his chest was gone. He and Brent had taken it easy up until now, but Scott was ready. He wanted all of Brent, and he intended to get it.

"Jesus," Scott groaned under his breath, losing track of what he was saying as Bret slid down him. He held his breath as Brent breached him for the first time, preparing him in the most deliciously hot way possible. Scott whimpered, unable to get enough, willing for more, and Brent delivered until he wasn't able to control himself any longer.

Brent got into position between his legs and looked down at him, eyes shining in the darkness. Scott wanted to see him more clearly but wasn't going to turn on the light and break the spell between them. Brent stroked his cheek and gently caressed his chin, his thumb tracing his lip as he pressed forward, Scott's body opening to him. Brent moved slowly, increasingly filling him by the second. It was wonderfully amazing, and Scott pressed forward, needing more. Brent stilled, a hand against his cheek, maintaining contact with him. Brent might not be able to talk to him in the conventional sense, but his hands and body spoke loud and clear.

Scott was cared for; every caress and movement told him that. Brent took such care with his touch and even the way they joined together, long and slow, filling and emptying, ecstasy building on top of passion. Scott could have told Brent what he wanted, but he just seemed to know.

"Oh God," Scott whimpered as Brent's hips pressed to his ass. He had all of Brent inside him, and he breathed shallowly, letting the stretch and burn wash over him and dissipate, followed by sheer joy as Brent slowly started to move. Nothing was tentative or hesitant. Brent leaned forward to kiss him, rocking his hips slowly, sending building ripples running through him. Almost instantly Scott needed release. Brent had him on the edge within minutes, and thankfully seemed to sense it, taking Scott's hands and holding them gently.

This was going to last, because Brent knew exactly what he was doing. Scott could feel that his pleasure was in Brent's control. Every movement was designed to either drive him mad or back him off, only so Brent could take him higher. Scott didn't know how to think; he'd never felt that way before, but his brain was now fried and all his senses centered on Brent. There was no one else, nothing else.

They rocked together, Brent completing him, sliding along that spot inside him, taking him to nirvana and back multiple times until nothing at all existed except Brent. Scott kept his eyes closed. There was nothing to see anyway, only to feel. Every nerve and sense had been reduced to the basest of feelings, and Scott wished this would never end. He was the center of the universe for a few minutes, until he could no longer hold back the tide of passion that slammed into him, carried him along like a surfer on a wave, then crashed over him in a cadence of release that left him unable to move.

Scott must have blacked out or transcended to another plane, maybe only for a fraction of a second, but it was enough of a glimpse of pure bliss for him to hold on to for the rest of his life.

"Brent," he whispered—at least he hoped so.

Brent stroked his arm, lying on the bed next to him. Scott didn't want to move, afraid everything would change and the world would be as it really was. Brent shifted slightly next to him and then rolled over, tugging Scott to him in a cocoon of heat in the otherwise cool, air-conditioned room. He lay still, wishing he could hear Brent's breathing and whispered intimacies, but that wasn't going to happen. Instead, Brent used his hands, caressing and loving on him in silence.

Scott's eyes filled with tears, and he lay still, hoping Brent wouldn't notice. Brent's caring embrace brought his emotions to the surface. He tried to stop them, but failed. He was going to spend the rest of his life in a world of silence.

Brent reached for his cheeks, gently caressed them, wiping away the tears, and held him a little tighter. Scott tried to imagine what Brent would tell him and came up with one thing: it was okay to cry and to mourn what he'd lost. Scott now had a pretty clear vision of what his life was going to be like. He was going to work, and he intended to live as fully and richly as possible. He had no intention of settling for second-best. So tonight, in safety, he was letting go of the past and would embrace the future full-on and without hesitation. Full speed ahead was his new motto. But first he had to say goodbye to the past, and that meant some tears and, thankfully, someone he... loved... to hold him.

As soon as that word entered his mind, it refused to leave. Scott was in love with Brent. Maybe he had been for a while. But how could he tell him? Not now. What if Brent didn't feel the same? What if he felt obligated to say it back? To stay? Scott would never want to trap him... ever.

SCOTT WOKE the following morning to an empty bed. He was a little surprised he'd slept through Brent getting up. Still, they didn't need to go anywhere, so maybe a lazy day would be good.

He inhaled and slipped out of bed, then pulled on his pants before following the rich scent of coffee to the kitchen.

Brent sat at the table with the newspaper laid out next to him. When Scott poured himself coffee and joined him, Brent stood to pull him into a hug, then kissed him hard enough that Scott nearly dropped the mug just because his head short-circuited within a few seconds. Damn.... Brent was an amazing kisser, and he held Scott so tightly. When he pulled away, Scott hugged Brent in return.

"I made some decisions last night," Scott told Brent without releasing him. "I need to accept that I'm going to live my life without being able to hear. I know it sounds dumb because I already signed up for classes, but I'm going to learn sign language and how to read lips and other people's expressions more clearly. I'm not going to sit around and wait for shit to happen. I'm going to *make* it happen." This was starting to feel like a mantra, and that was good.

Brent pulled back, smiling. Scott already knew he had his support.

"I do want to know who hit me and why they just drove away. When the police do catch this guy—" The image of Spencer came to mind, nervous like he was at the garage the day before. "—I want to look him in the eye and ask him why he drove away. What in the hell made him think that he could just leave someone like that, to potentially die?" Scott clenched his fists. "You need to promise you'll be there with me."

"I will, but why?" At least that's what Scott thought Brent said.

"Because my mom and dad will try to shelter me. Just like James said they would. They're already trying to run interference for anything that might upset me. I see them talking when they think I'm not looking. I know they mean well." He paused. "I need you to be strong for me if you can."

That's when Scott saw the shadow of doubt pass over Brent's features, that dark cloud that didn't stay for very long but was enough for Scott to wonder once again what had happened to him.

"What if I can't?" Brent asked.

Scott pulled away, turned toward the bedroom, then back toward Brent. "You mean, you won't?" He didn't understand at all.

Brent shuffled to the coffee table and grabbed a pad. He wrote, then handed it to Scott, who sat on the sofa.

No. I mean what if I can't. I'm not good with that sort of thing. I want to help you, and I'll do what I can, but…. I'll stand by you in every way I can.

Brent flopped down on the sofa, wrapping his arms around himself. His expression lightened as though he had made up his mind about something important.

Scott sat still, watching Brent, hoping he'd tell him whatever was behind this notion of his that he was weak. Scott had never seen that himself. He always saw Brent as someone who stood up for him and was a good friend, a good manager, and who really seemed to care for him.

"I told you before that you don't need to tell me what happened if you don't want to. But I think you might need to tell someone. If not me, then talk to James or Trevor. They'll understand—I know they will. But whatever happened that gave you this image of yourself… you have to talk about it."

Brent shook his head as he wrote. He crumpled the page he'd written on and tossed it in the trash. Scott stood, pulled it out, and smoothed the page so he could read the words.

You'll never look at me the same way again if I do.

"Why would I do that?" Scott sat next to Brent again and leaned forward. "Don't you understand that I see you? I know you for who you are. I've watched you for two damn years while we danced around each other and were too stupid to actually do anything. You know my fears and worries. You get me to share them with you. But you keep holding back. Don't you trust me?" He knew he was pushing and that it could very well backfire in a way that made Brent close himself off even more, but he needed to get through to him.

I'm a coward, Brent wrote, cringing as he showed Scott the page.

Scott shook his head firmly. "You know there's a difference between avoiding a fight and running away from one."

Brent leaned back, writing once again. *How about hiding from one? I know who I am and I've had to accept it. It's part of what's inside me, and as much as I hate it, I can't turn away from it. I can't undo what I've done.* His shoulders slumped and he looked at the floor, growing paler by the second.

Scott grew worried. This wasn't the guy he thought he knew. Brent was usually confident and caring. He ran the garage like it was a family, and he'd been there for him since the accident more than anyone else. Seeing Brent looking as though he wanted to disappear into the ground was a total shock.

"What happened, Brent?" Scott asked, scooting next to him, putting his arms around his chest in order to try to comfort him. But it didn't seem to be working. Waves of tension washed over Brent, becoming more and more intense by the second. Scott wished he'd kept his mouth shut, but he'd wanted to help. Instead, it looked like he'd made things harder.

Brent reached for the pad, wrote, and then handed him the page. *My dad died because of me, because I was a coward.* Brent turned away, then stood, went to the bedroom, and closed the door.

"Dammit," Scott swore, knowing he'd pushed too hard and driven Brent away. He wondered what the hell he should do now and thought he should just go home. As Scott reached into his pocket to pull out his phone, he thought of texting his mother to come get him. He typed the message he wanted and sent it with a small sigh, not sure what else to do.

CHAPTER 7

BRENT SAT on the side of his bed, berating himself. He'd only proven once again that he was truly a coward. He fled to his room instead of dealing with the problem straight on. Scott had given him a chance to man up, but he'd run away to hide. That was his fucking pattern, and he hated it and himself for it.

"Shit!" He didn't want to talk about his past, and yet he fucking knew Scott was right and he needed to. He'd always been so full of advice to help Scott, but did he take it when it was offered to him? Hell no—he ran away and hid in his room like he was still ten years old and scared of thunderstorms. All he had to do was go back out there, but then how was he going to face Scott? Brent covered his face with his hands and wished he'd been a better person, one who could just stand up to what he'd done, face it down, and have it over with. That was what he needed.

Brent stood and forced his feet to the door. He pulled it open and stepped out, heat high in his cheeks. Scott sat on the sofa, looking at him, his expression hard and his eyes filled with concern. Brent wasn't sure what to say or how to go about it, so he shoved his hands in his pockets. Scott got up and walked past him into the bedroom. Brent turned and watched as Scott finished dressing. Then Scott returned to the sofa, sat back down, and crossed his arms over his chest.

What's going on? Brent wrote, then brought the page over to the sofa. Something wasn't right, and Scott was most definitely angry with him. Well, maybe angry wasn't the right word. Disappointed? Hell, he was disappointed in himself, but that was a recurring theme. Had been for a long time now.

"I sent a message and I'm waiting."

When Scott turned away, Brent sighed. He really had blown it. Hell, he should have known it was only a matter of time. He hadn't even been able to be there for his father, so why had he thought he was good enough for Scott?

The bell rang, and Brent buzzed them in, figuring it was Carolyn to come pick Scott up. He opened the door a few seconds later and was shocked as Trevor and James stepped inside.

"Scott messaged us and said that you needed some help," James said, his arm on Trevor's.

Scott came right over to hug James and then Trevor before turning to Brent. "You and I need to have a talk, and since you didn't want to talk to me, I figured I'd turn the tables. You brought in the big guns when I was feeling sorry for myself, so I thought it was my turn." He crossed his arms over his chest, his expression firm. "Think of this as an intervention."

"Shit," Brent grumbled under his breath.

"Buddy, you're one of my oldest friends, and in all that time, you've never said anything about your dad other than he was dead. It's like there's a wall around it and you refuse to let anyone in. So it's time you let that down." Trevor turned to James, who was nodding along. Brent was being overpowered, and damn it all if he could stand up to the three of them. "You know we all care, so unwind this chain that's wrapped around your waist and let it go."

James felt his way over to wrap his arms around Brent. "Even I can tell that it weighs on you. What have you got to lose?"

"Only the fact that everyone I know will have proof that I'm a loser." Brent couldn't stand up to this onslaught, and motioned to the chairs. Everyone might as well get comfortable.

Trevor helped James over to a chair, and James searched for the table with his hands. Then he set up his tablet and had Scott adjust it so he could see the screen. Apparently he was going to act as interpreter.

"I'm not comfortable with this."

"I know," Trevor told him. "But think of it this way. Scott cares about you enough to call us and risk your wrath because he wants to help you. This isn't some deep-seated curiosity on his part. This is hurting you. He can feel it, as can the rest of us. Do you remember a few months ago when those guys tried to rob the garage? You did what they asked and then notified the police. But you beat yourself up over it for weeks. I didn't understand it. You followed my instructions and did what was right, but you still felt like shit."

"I should have stood up to them—instead, I nearly crapped myself." Brent turned away. "I'm just a huge coward."

"No, you aren't. You kept a cool head, did what they wanted, got a good look at them, and the police caught them and recovered the money within a few hours. Think about it. Those boys could have hurt Lee, Scott, or anyone else. They were out of their minds on crack and dipshitness. You brought the incident to an end with no one getting hurt. What is wrong with that?" Trevor caught him in his gaze, and Brent walked around the table to sit next to Scott on the sofa. It looked like they weren't going to let him off the hook.

"Why do you feel that you're a coward?" Scott asked as he handed him back the sheet of paper from earlier. "Please tell me."

Brent nodded and tried to get his thoughts together. "I was fourteen. I remember that day like it was yesterday, because I see it all the time in my dreams." He waited while James typed. "My dad was with the Milwaukee Police Department. He was a detective, and I was really proud of him."

"I didn't know that," Trevor said softly.

"Because I never talk about it. He worked on lots of cases and was good at his job. At least that's what everyone told me. Anyway, I wanted to go swimming, and Dad said he'd take me to one of the park pools. They had waterslides and diving boards, and I really wanted to go, so he took me. It was supposed to be one of those things we did together. It was about five, I guess.

Dad said we'd go late so we didn't get sunburned. Anyway, we both had suits on and he brought me over. We went swimming, and as usual, he and I had a lot of fun." Brent turned away, looking toward the kitchen. Anywhere but at them. "My dad and I…. He was so special. Other kids used to beg for attention. Dad and I loved doing stuff together." He wiped his eyes. Brent had already cried over losing his dad so many times, he wasn't going to do it again.

"The pool was closing, so we'd changed and left the area, heading to the car. My birthday had been the week before, and Dad had gotten me a pair of Jordans and the coolest clothes because I'd asked him for them. So I was wearing them, and some kid came up to us with a knife. As soon as he got close, my dad pushed me behind him and started talking to the kid, who threatened him if I didn't hand over my shoes."

Brent groaned and thought about how to continue. "Dad handed me the keys and said to get in the car, lock the doors, and if I had to, drive away. Dad had started teaching me how to drive, at least the basics, so I knew what to do. I got in as Dad continued talking to the kid, and I did as Dad said, locking the doors. I got the keys in the engine, my hands shaking, and turned it on. I thought my dad was going to get in, so I waited to unlock the doors. We could get away then. There was a radio in the car, so I used it, trying to call for help.

"I turned back to Dad to try to tell him that I had help on the way, and the guy lunged for him. I could hear him screaming. He was probably seventeen and he… he…." Brent was afraid to close his eyes. If he did, he'd see it all over again. "The guy tore into my dad. There was blood all over the windows, and I sat in there, screaming, and crawled down onto the floor of the car. I was too afraid to move. There was blood everywhere. My dad's blood."

Brent shook. Scott stayed still and then hugged him. "None of this is your fault."

"Bullshit. I hid in the car as that guy cut my dad to pieces. He wasn't on duty and was just another guy, and I hid while my dad died. By the time help got there, he was gone. Dad was dead, and the guy had run off. They caught him, but I was… I had to go to court and tell everyone how I was too scared to help my dad." Brent buried his face in his hands.

"What about your mom? What does she say?"

Brent shook his head. "What was she supposed to say? She's my mom and has always said it wasn't my fault. That I did the right thing, but all she was afraid of was that I'd have been killed too."

The room remained silent, only broken by the sound of keys clicking softly as James typed.

"Maybe she's right. You could have been killed. This guy took out an experienced police officer. He was dangerous, probably high. Your dad knew that and wanted to protect you. That was his first thought."

"But he was my dad." Why didn't they understand? "I saw him die, and I did nothing. He was the most important person in my life, and I cowered on the floor while he was killed and then the man who did it ran away. At least that's what they told me once they got me out of the car. I was too scared to move, so they had to carry me out of the car and to an ambulance." Brent shook, and Scott held him tighter. "I looked back and saw my dad's body on the ground. He was on his side and was covered in blood. I screamed and tried to get to him, but everyone just shook their heads. They did the best they could for me, but I knew, I've always known, that I cowered while some asshole killed my dad. I should have helped him. I should have been there for him the way he always was for me. And I wasn't." Brent sighed, his throat dry. He coughed and couldn't stop. Trevor went to the kitchen and brought him a glass of water. Brent drank half of it down and set it on the coffee table.

"Did they get you counseling?" Scott asked.

"God, yes," Brent answered. "I saw shrinks and doctors for years. They were useless. One tried to get me to talk about my dad and tell him what sort of tension there was between us, like my dad and I hated each other. I called him a quack, and when they made me see him again and he asked the same stupid questions, I kicked him in the shin and I never went back. I wish I'd gotten him in the nuts." The others tittered, and Brent figured they thought he was kidding. "I was a scared, messed-up kid. I'd seen my dad killed in front of me, and all this ass could think to do was get me to talk about the issues I had with him. Mom took me to others, and they all tried to help me, but nothing worked but time, I guess."

Scott shook his head. "I don't think that helped you much."

Brent gasped and looked at the others, who all nodded slowly. "What the hell? I dealt with it and was able to move on. What the fuck else was I supposed to do?" His words looked even harsher when he saw them on the tablet screen.

"Because you have this idea in your head that you're a coward. You're carrying so much guilt with you. And you did nothing wrong." Scott held his hands. "Did you ever talk to your mom about all this?"

"Why?" Brent shook his head. "My mom lost her husband. For a long time, she was just trying to get through the day, the same as me. I always felt like I let her down because she lost Dad too." His stomach lurched, and he hoped to hell he wasn't going to throw up. "There's nothing I can do about any of this. The past is the past. Everyone has told me that. I've tried to be the best person I can, and I've been there for my mom." He was so happy to see her getting out again. He drank some more water. "I've told you guys my biggest secret and—"

Trevor stood and leaned over him. "Dude. I can't begin to think about what you went through and how all that affected you as a kid. But you're an adult now, and you can be whoever you want." He pulled Brent to his feet and hugged him hard. "You've been my best friend for a long time, and I'm torn between hugging the hell out of you and smacking you around for not telling me. I'll hug you right now, but the smacking around may come later." Trevor hugged him closer.

"Thanks." Brent smiled to himself.

"But you better listen to me," Trevor added in his boss voice. "This whole 'I'm a coward' thing you have going on is a bunch of crap. I've never thought that, and neither has anyone else. Dean doesn't think that either. It's all in your head." He stepped back, and James took his place, the slighter man hugging him surprisingly tightly.

"We can rarely control the way others think, but we definitely control what we say to ourselves." James hugged him again before backing away. Trevor put his arms around James's waist, holding him tenderly.

"He's right," Trevor added.

"This whole coward story you've got going on is a load of shit, and you need to write a different one for inside your head." Scott glared at him, crossing his arms over his chest. Dang, he really meant business.

Be that as it may, it was so much easier for others to tell him to change, but he knew he was right. The past couldn't be changed—he'd done what he'd done and nothing was going to make it go away.

"Do you guys want a snack or something?" It was too early in the day for a beer, but Brent wanted one badly. Hell, he had a case in the pantry—maybe he should put it in the refrigerator so he could drink it later and forget this entire conversation. Brent knew his friends meant well, but nothing was going to change… not really.

Brent got to his feet and went to the kitchen. He hunted up some cheese, crackers, and salami, putting it on a plate. He also got some sodas and juice and then brought everything to the coffee table, hoping it was okay.

"You know this attempt at changing the subject isn't going to work," James said.

"Damn, and I thought I could distract all of you with cheese."

"Okay, you can distract me. I love cheese." James reached for the plate while Trevor whispered directions so James would know what was where. Then Trevor opened a can of soda and pressed it into James's hand. "See, it worked great, and this is really good cheese. Where did you get it?"

Trevor rolled his eyes, and James chuckled while eating his cracker and cheese. "That's enough of that." He leaned forward, fixing his gaze on Brent. "You really need to get over this thing."

Brent sighed. He was becoming tired of all this pretty quickly. Yes, they were his friends, and he loved them all dearly, but they were getting on his nerves. He wasn't going to be able to change the way his mind worked, and his opinion of himself, in a matter of hours.

"Okay. I think we've harped on this enough. He knows what we think of him, and I hope he'll listen to us and take it to heart." Trevor turned to him, his eyes hard. "We are telling you the truth. This isn't us blowing smoke up your ass because you're our friend. Hell, if we thought you were a coward or an asshole, we'd say so, because that's the kind of people we are."

James typed as he tried not to laugh. He failed, and what came across on the screen was a bunch of garbage that James had to correct. Then Scott laughed, and what the hell, Brent tried not to because he really wanted to feel pissy about this whole thing, but he laughed too. Trevor wasn't the kind of guy to sugarcoat things, and neither was James. They were both good guys, but sometimes too truthful for their own good.

"Thanks for that. I promise I'll give it some thought." Brent rolled his eyes. "Can we talk about something other than my personality flaws for a little while?"

"But that's so much fun," Scott quipped as soon as James typed his question. "And it's better than a review of my flaws, which my mother seems to find fascinating." He scratched the top of his head. "As an example, it's Sunday morning and I stayed out all night with my boyfriend. I'm surprised she hasn't been messaging me about going to church with them. She never gives up, I swear." Scott picked up his phone, then chuckled, needing to correct his statement. He did have a message from her. Scott answered it and set his phone down again.

"How about lunch?" James suggested, after checking his talking watch, which told him in its mechanical voice that it was eleven thirty-one aaay emmm.

Brent agreed, emotionally drained. "We'll get changed and can go in a few minutes." He guided Scott into the bedroom and sat on the edge of the bed. All he wanted was a few minutes to himself. This hadn't turned out to be the great morning he'd been hoping for. Still, he felt a little lighter. The three of them knew his deepest regret and hadn't condemned him for it. Granted, Brent had done plenty of that on his own.

Scott sat next to him, holding his hand.

"I really thought you'd…." Brent stopped. He didn't have a pad, and Scott wasn't going to hear him anyway. But he'd really thought Scott would think less of him after he'd confessed about his dad.

"Stop beating yourself up for something that happened so long ago. I know you've been carrying that a long time, but you didn't have to. You didn't do anything wrong, and you aren't a coward." Scott leaned close to him and held him tightly.

Brent wanted to believe him, he really did. But unfortunately he'd seen nothing to alter his view.

BRENT AND Scott joined Trevor and James for lunch at a small diner-type restaurant just a few blocks away. As they were eating, Scott handed Brent his vibrating phone.

"Hello?"

He was greeted with a throat clearing softly. "I'm trying to reach Scott Spearman," a deep voice said, and instantly Brent was suspicious. "I'm Officer Graves with the Brown Deer Police Department. Can I speak with him?"

"I'm Brent Berkheimer, his boyfriend. Scott can't hear. He is right next to me and I can relay a message to him." Brent's stomach clenched with worry, and he shared a glance with Scott.

Papers rustled in the background. "Oh. Yes. I see that. I should have looked deeper into the file. Right. The lieutenant asked me to call with an update. We were able to match the paint from Scott's car to the one discovered at Wilson's Body Shop."

"Damn...," Brent said softly. He would have liked the person who had hit Scott to have been someone he didn't know. "So, it was Spencer Phillips who hit Scott?" He had to ask.

"He is the owner of the car, yes. We will be talking to him today. We wanted to tell Scott that we are getting close to an answer about what happened."

"Thank you." Suddenly Brent's worries and old issues didn't seem too important. "I will relay what you told me." He hung up and pulled the pad from his pocket so he could tell Scott what he'd been told.

Scott turned pale and set down his fork. He stared blankly at the wall for a few seconds, then pushed his chair back and hurried toward the back of the diner, with Brent right behind him. By the time Brent closed the bathroom door, the sound of Scott's heaving filled the small room. He wanted to punch the wall on Scott's behalf. He was so angry and hurt for him that it brought tears to his eyes. "Dammit." He wiped them with the back of his hand. Brent hated seeing Scott upset.

Brent wet a couple of paper towels and handed them to Scott when he came out. He wished he had words of comfort, but held him instead, letting Scott shake. "It's going to be okay." It didn't matter if Scott could hear him or not. Somehow Brent was going to make it so Scott was okay.

Scott shifted a few times, wiping his face. "We should join them again. There isn't anything more we can do right now. This is up to the police." He sounded so reasonable, but Brent heard the distress in his tone and saw the worry in his eyes. "Maybe then this can finally be over."

Brent nodded and let Scott go first. They returned to the table, and Brent took a drink of water but didn't touch the last of his stir-fry. Not that anyone could blame him for a second.

Trevor insisted on getting the check once they were done, so Brent took Scott out to the car and started the engine to cool off the interior. He grabbed a notepad and pen, wrote, and handed it to Scott.

Do you want me to take you home? Your mom and dad should be back from church.

"No." Scott turned to look out the window. "I need to go somewhere I can think." He turned back to Brent, his eyes welling. "Can you take me to the waterwheel?"

Brent nodded and drove to the park. He led Scott through the woods and along the path to the little stream. Brent sat on the log bench as Scott paced back and forth, muttering under his breath. Brent caught a few words here and there, but mostly he felt the frustration washing off Scott in waves. Eventually the muttering died away and the pacing slowed until Scott sat next to him, tugging his shirt off, golden skin covered in a sheen of sweat.

"I don't know how someone who was my friend could do that… to anyone." Scott's shoulders slumped and he sighed loudly. "Do you have any idea?"

Brent nodded. "Sometimes people suck." He made sure Scott could see him, and the smile he got told him Scott understood what he'd said. "You're getting good at reading lips."

Scott moved closer. "Just yours."

Brent cupped Scott's chin and kissed him. "I hate that you're going through this." He repeated what he'd said slowly, and Scott nodded.

"I hate it too. Shit, if it was a stranger, it would be easier to take." He turned away, and they both watched the water as it sluiced over the wheel. Scott shifted to him, leaning against his shoulder, and then buried his face. "I thought he was my friend once and… I didn't do anything wrong."

No, he hadn't. Not from what Scott had told him. There were two sides to every story, but he didn't deserve any of this. No one did.

"Everyone at church is going to take his side. He and his family do so much for them. They'll say I did something wrong and somehow caused the accident because I sat at the light for too long or something."

Brent put his arms around Scott and held him, letting him get this out.

"I don't suppose it matters since I'm not going there anymore." He got comfortable next to Brent, who shifted but left his arms around him, and they watched the water for a while. The breeze rustled the trees overhead, which cast changing patterns of light over the ground at their feet. He breathed deeply, hoping to calm Scott and help him feel better, somehow. Brent wasn't sure if what he was doing was helping, but he had to try. Sometimes the hardest things in life were dealing with the things one had no control over at all.

Brent kissed the top of Scott's head. "I love you," he whispered. Brent's heart hurt when Scott's hurt, and his heart leaped when Scott smiled. He thought of Scott first thing in the morning, and Scott was his final thought before he went to bed.

"Brent…. We can go when you're ready."

Brent wasn't sure where to take him. He didn't want to just go back to the apartment, so he made sure his mom was home. They walked hand in hand back to the car, and he drove to his mom's, knowing she'd have something decadent to eat. Nothing helped heal whatever ailed him like one of his mother's pies.

HIS MOTHER was awesome, fussing over Scott just the way Brent knew she would.

"Would you like another piece of pie?" his mother asked, pointing to the half-empty tin, already moving to slice it.

"No, thank you. It was delicious, but two slices is my limit." Scott smiled broadly enough that the lines reached his eyes, and she patted his hand before lifting the pot of coffee. Brent swore they were both going to float out of the kitchen if they drank any more.

"I'm so happy you came by. I was hoping to meet you." His mom spoke a little loudly, and Brent smiled. She was doing her best. Brent passed her a pad, and she wrote before handing the note across the table. *You come by any time. I love a man with a good appetite.* She leaned back and turned to Brent. "I love seeing you happy."

"I like being happy and thank you… for being you." He leaned close, kissing her cheek. "I love you." She kissed his cheek in return and did the same to Scott. They both stood and Brent took the dishes to the sink before hugging his mother. Her brand of care was just what they'd needed.

Then Brent took Scott home, and they explained to his parents what they'd been told by the police. After giving Scott a kiss goodbye, Brent went to his apartment and spent the rest of the evening wishing he'd asked Scott to come back with him. He missed his companionship. Without Scott, his place felt empty and too damn quiet. Scott filled Brent's apartment and his life with sound and life.

Brent didn't sleep well at all, worried about Scott and wondering if he was okay. So in the morning, he went into the garage early and got busy. By the time the guys began arriving,

Brent had most of the week-ending paperwork done and faxed over to the accountant's office.

Lee's mom brought him into work, and Scott pulled in a few minutes later using his mother's car. He and Lee got right to work. Brent checked the appointments and handed out the jobs until everyone was busy.

Then, with little to do, he sat in his office, watching Scott as he bent over the hood of a car, his work jumpsuit pulling tight. God, Brent had never thought of those things as sexy, but dammit, they were on Scott. "Shit." He turned away, forcing his mind back on the job, because he was not supposed to perv on his boyfriend when they were working.

"How are things going?" Trevor asked as he opened the door and strode into the office.

"Great. Our appointment book is full, and I have some guys coming in at five to work a few hours this evening. Darryl is going to come in to supervise them. But it's the only way we can stay current with the appointments."

Trevor grinned and opened the roll of paper he'd been carrying. "I've been thinking of adding another service bay. This one is specifically for oil changes and tire rotations. That way we can free up the guys for other work. We've recovered from Alan's theft of a few years ago and it's time to reinvest in the business. I have the land to add another bay, but that's all the room there is."

"The guys on second are part-timers who need some extra money. A couple of them worked at Sears for years, and with hours being cut back there, the guys need some extra cash. I bet they'd be willing to work full-time once we have the space for them."

"Good. I can put these plans in motion, but it's going to take a while."

"We'll make the most of what we have." Brent looked out the window when he heard yelling, then jumped to his feet. One of the men from church stood toe to toe with Lee, who was right in front of Scott. Brent raced out.

"You going to hit a blind guy? How is that going to look to all your friends?" Lee's jaw was set and he looked as ferocious as a tiger. "About as smart as yelling at a deaf man."

"What's going on?" Brent bellowed, and the stranger turned toward him. He remembered this guy from the gyro restaurant and church.

"Marshall came to talk to me, I think." Scott was paler than he had been after the cops called.

"I'm calling the police," Brent said as he turned toward the office.

"Get away," Marshall yelled, pushing Lee aside hard enough that he tumbled to the floor. Marshall grabbed Scott in a choke hold. Scott gasped, and the garage went completely quiet, all eyes shifting to where Marshall held Scott.

"What the hell is wrong with you?" Brent shouted, spinning back around.

"Don't get too close or I'll toss him into this pit headfirst!"

Brent looked back at the office, where Trevor was hanging up the phone. "The police are already on their way. Whatever you've got running through your head, it isn't going to work." He kept his voice as level and as calm as he could. "So what's the deal?"

"He ruined everything!" Marshall shouted, shaking Scott, who held Marshall's arm from his throat. "He always did. First, he makes a pass at Spencer, who was supposed to be mine. He was supposed to love me! But instead, Spencer goes for the little queen here and then freaks out because someone might find out." Marshall pulled Scott tighter against his body.

"That's no reason to hurt him. Just walk away, man. You aren't in this too deep yet." God, if he released Scott, Brent would let Marshall drive away for all he cared. The police could pick him up later, once he'd calmed down.

"Bullshit! Spencer turned me in, the bastard. He ratted me out. Spencer said it would be all right, that no one would know that I borrowed his car. He'd never tell anyone, and he'd get his cousin to get the car fixed on the down-low. No one would ask any questions and everything would be fine!"

Brent blinked and took a step closer. "*You* hit Scott?"

"Yeah. I hit him. It was late and I saw his car. He pulled to a stop, and I figured I'd hit him, give him a scare. Maybe get him frightened enough he'd leave town. Put the fear of God in the little ass-rider. How in the fuck was I supposed to know that he'd go through the windshield and shit?" Marshall yanked upward, and Scott gasped, his breathing labored.

Brent knew that he was only going to get one chance and that Scott was going to be hurt badly if he didn't act. He saw Lee, standing where Marshall couldn't see him, pick up some wrenches off a workbench. Brent's stomach fluttered, and he wondered if he could do this. Did he have the fucking guts?

Lee dropped the wrenches, the clang filling the garage. Marshall jumped and turned away. Brent didn't hesitate. All he thought about was Scott. He leaped, grabbed Marshall's arm, and wrenched it away from Scott, who fell to the ground.

"You stupid son of a bitch!" Anger welled, and Brent's fist connected with Marshall's jaw, sending him back.

Trevor barreled out of the office, tackled Marshall linebacker-style, and pulled him to the ground just before he would have fallen into the pit.

"Get the hell off me!" Marshall screamed, thrashing as Trevor held him down.

Brent hurried to Scott and helped him up.

"I'm okay," Scott gasped, rubbing his throat. "He didn't hurt me too bad."

Sirens sounded, getting closer, as Brent led Scott into the office and got him seated. "Lee, you were amazing," Brent called out, sticking his head around the corner. "That was brilliant."

"That was awesome, the way you came to my rescue," Scott said.

Brent got him a glass of water, and once Scott got a drink, he proceeded to check Scott over to make sure there were no other injuries. As soon as he was done, Brent tugged Scott into a hug and held him tight.

"See, you aren't a coward." Scott held him in return as Trevor spoke to the police outside. Brent let Trevor do as much of the explaining as possible. After all, they had all heard what Marshall had confessed to. Not only had he hit Scott, but he'd done it on purpose. He'd known Scott's car and hadn't cared what happened to him. If it were possible, Brent would like to go back out there and beat the shit out of Marshall all over again.

"Guys, the police want to talk to you," Trevor said, sticking his head inside.

Brent patted Scott on the shoulder. *Stay here*, he wrote on the blotter and went out.

The police had Marshall in the back of one of the cars, and Brent explained what had happened. "The bastard was responsible for the accident that hurt Scott. It left him permanently deaf. He not only admitted to hitting him, but that he did it on purpose to scare him." Brent was so angry, he could hardly see straight. The entire building seemed to have been painted red for a few seconds, and so help him, he'd tear anyone who countered him limb from limb. He closed his eyes to calm down. He needed to get it under control. They were okay and Marshall was in custody. Steady breathing.

"We all heard him," Trevor said, and the others nodded.

"We need to speak with Scott," an officer said.

"He's deaf, so you'll need pad and pen."

"I'm able to sign," the officer said.

"Scott became deaf a few weeks ago, when Marshall hit him. We're signed up for classes, but he doesn't sign yet."

Brent went into the office and brought out Scott, who had an awkward conversation with the police explaining how Marshall had held him, where he knew him from, as well as filling in their past.

"He's a huge closet case of some sort," Scott said. "He and I used to be friends some time ago."

"We'll need you both to come down to the station and give statements so we can charge him officially. We're also going to talk to everyone here as witnesses."

"Of course," Trevor said. "Just let these people go back to their jobs. They have things they need to do. If they don't work, they don't get paid." It might have sounded harsh, but every one of the mechanics got paid based on the jobs they finished, and if they stood around, they didn't get paid.

They returned to work, and Trevor said the police could use the office for interviews if they needed to. There were a lot of questions that Brent answered. The hardest part was when they talked to Lee and to Scott. They were both half lost, and Brent was grateful Scott couldn't hear one officer's tone, because he tried to make things sound like Scott had done something wrong.

"Let me get one thing straight," Brent said, stepping forward. "I have a shop full of witnesses who will testify that Scott was a victim. He did nothing to provoke this kind of hatred, and he was the one getting choked."

"We need to get to the truth," the officer said harshly.

"The truth is that you will back off. I'll be in touch with your superiors, and this attitude will be noted in your record. My dad was a detective with Milwaukee PD. He taught me a lot about how the police should act, and treating a victim like a criminal isn't on that list. You have a confession that can be corroborated by at least eight people. So I think you have an open-and-shut case. I suggest you go with that."

"But all this boils down to some homosexual love spat," he sniped.

"No, it does not. Marshall is a criminal and confessed to using his vehicle as a weapon. That's assault with a deadly weapon. Anything else that happened was years ago, and I suggest you keep that in mind."

"Brent," Trevor cautioned, and Brent stepped away, his temper flaring. "It's all right. I've already called the chief, and he'll be over in a few minutes." Trevor grinned evilly, and the officer paled to a ghostly white. "I don't know what personal agenda you have going on, but it will come to an end."

"How do you know the chief?" Brent asked.

"James's parents. I met him at one of their parties." Trevor crossed his arms over his chest. "So now are we through here? Can I tell him there was a misunderstanding, or leave it alone and he'll be on his way over?"

"I think we're good," the second officer said, glaring at his partner. "We have what we need. Just come down to the station to review and sign your statements tomorrow morning, and we'll be able to file charges against him, as well as the car's owner for aiding and abetting."

"Thank you." Trevor shook his hand. "I'll call the chief to tell him he isn't needed here." Brent had no doubt that Trevor and the chief would be having a conversation about Officer Asshole in any event. Trevor wasn't one to let this sort of thing go.

Since the officers had all they needed, they left with Marshall in custody.

"I didn't see that coming at all. I thought it was Spencer." Scott sat down, and Brent sat next to him. Brent took the time to fill him in on everything that had been said, keeping the notepad where Scott could see it as he wrote. "You mean he did it on purpose?" Scott began shaking.

That's what he said, and we all heard him. Brent held Scott's hand, knowing Scott had wondered if that was possible. They'd all discounted it and it had turned out to be real.

"The idiot really tried to kill me?" Scott squeezed Brent's hand.

Brent shook his head. *I don't think so.* He wrote quickly. *I think he wanted to scare you so you'd leave town. He wanted you gone. I think in his mind you stole Spencer from him, because after you two were caught, Spencer backed away and went so deep in the closet that Marshall's hopes were dashed as well. He hated you for that.* It was convoluted logic to Brent, but it must have made sense to Marshall. The guy couldn't be completely balanced if he was willing to use a car as a battering ram to hurt someone else.

"So he's in love with Spencer?" Scott asked, clearly confused.

That's what it sounded like, and he blames you for not getting what he wanted. The hatred has been festering for years. Brent let Scott read before continuing. *This has nothing to do with you and everything to do with him.*

Scott shook his head. "You know Marshall is married. I always wondered why anyone would marry him, and now I know she must have been desperate. Either that or she wanted the prestige of marrying into his family. It can't because Marshall is some great husband." Scott rolled his eyes.

Who knows. Brent shrugged and continued writing. *He's obviously living a lie, and they're taking it out on you and I suspect on anyone else who might be different. They're all so afraid of themselves that they can't tolerate anyone who might remind them of what they're hiding.* Brent paused before writing his last thought. *You must have been a regular reminder for that resentment to have lasted so long.* He set the page down and pulled Scott to him. Brent needed to hold Scott as much as he needed to be held in return. Marshall having Scott in his arms that way, threatening him, had scared the crap out of him, but it had also helped him see some things clearly. But now wasn't the time to talk about them.

"I think I need to go back to work," Scott said softly. "I can sit here all day and run things over in my head, or I can try to be productive." He didn't make any move to pull away, and Brent stayed where he was, perfectly content. Brent wasn't able to tell Scott what he wanted at the moment. That would require letting Scott go, and he had no intention of doing that. Eventually Scott stepped away, and Brent let his arms settle at his sides.

Scott went up on his tiptoes to kiss him, then left the office. "I'll see you after work and we can talk," he said with a grin and a wink when he poked his head back into the office. "Don't worry. I'll be okay."

Brent wondered if he should call Scott's parents, because maybe that whole ordeal had fried Scott's brains. He should be very worried, but given everything Scott had been through in the past few weeks, he was beginning to think that Scott had a set of brass balls, which was attractive as hell.

Brent sat at his desk, trying to do something other than fret about the past few hours. He still had a little work to do, and while tension and residual excitement still electrified the air, the guys were getting back to work and Brent needed to do the same.

But he couldn't. Over the last six weeks or so, he'd come damn close to losing Scott twice, and both times it had felt like his heart had stopped and was never going to restart again. Forget about CPR—that kind of damage was going to be permanent. The simple fact was that he was in love, completely and totally, head over heels, put-himself-in-danger in love with Scott. Just the thought of it was enough to make him smile after one of the shittiest days he'd ever had. Now Brent had to figure out what the hell he was going to do about it. He'd whispered "I love you" to Scott, but a hell of a lot of good that had done. Scott couldn't hear him, and words completely fell short. Brent had no intention of writing that he loved Scott on a piece of scrap paper and placing it in front of him, the way he did when he gave him special instructions on engine work to be completed. He rolled his eyes at the very notion. No, he needed to come up with something that truly expressed how he was feeling and what he really wanted to say.

"Where are you?" Trevor asked from behind him. Brent hadn't even noticed him come into the office, he was so deep in his own thoughts.

"Sorry." Brent colored and turned to the papers on his desk. He wasn't being paid to woolgather.

"You were long gone. Was it the attack?" Trevor closed the door to the office.

"No." Brent had always been able to talk to Trevor about just about anything. There was no need to hold back now. "I need to figure out a way to tell Scott something very important." He scratched his head. "In this case actions speak louder than words, and I need to figure out what I want to do."

Trevor patted him on the shoulder, grinning. "I know."

"How?"

"Because you're right. Actions do speak louder than words. And you said plenty this afternoon, whether you know it or not." Trevor's smile was summer-sun bright.

Chapter 8

Damn it all. He'd wanted to go back to Brent's after work, but as soon as he told his mom and dad what had happened, they had swooped in and insisted he come home. Not that he could blame them. They were freaked and had their legs knocked out from under them by the fact that someone they knew from church could act like this.

"Mom, I'm fine," Scott told her for the eighth time. "Marshall didn't stand a chance. Not against Brent and all the guys at the garage." He smiled as best he could from where he sat on the sofa, leaning forward to take her hand while his dad fidgeted nervously in the other chair.

We don't understand how you can be so calm, his father said in a note.

"Because. See, you weren't there. Yes, I was scared, but I kept calm, and Brent looked like a man possessed. I don't know everything that happened, but you should have seen Brent! Marshall had me around the neck, and when he turned, Brent sailed across the floor—I thought he'd sprouted wings. Marshall loosened his grip, and I fell to the floor. Brent took it from there. It was beautiful. Then Trevor got him and held him down until the police got there." He grinned widely. "It was totally awesome. Well, not the being held and choked part, but that way they stood up for me."

We're just worried, his dad said in another note, and his mother's hands shook in his.

"Maybe. But it's over. Marshall isn't going anywhere, and even if his folks bail him out...." Scott really didn't want to think about that. "This whole thing started because of Marshall.

He's… well, the guy is pretty messed up in the head. The one I feel sorry for is his wife. Darlene deserves so much better than him and the mess he created." He shook his head. "I really wish I could help her."

His mother turned to his dad, and the two of them had a conversation that Scott didn't catch, which really pissed him off.

"I am in the room, and it's rude to talk around me." He released his mother's soft hands and leaned back. "You've been doing that a lot and you think I don't see it, but I do. If you're going to talk about me, then do so in a way I can understand." He stood and walked to the opening to the kitchen. "I'm going to get a snack. You talk all you want. At least I won't be able to fucking see you." He stalked out. One thing was for sure—not being able to hear meant he got the last word.

Well, at least until his father stormed in under a head of steam. He crossed his arms over his chest, glaring at Scott.

"I can't hear you…." Scott knew he was being a shit, but he needed to make a point. He turned away and pulled a bowl of strawberries out of the refrigerator, sat at the table, and popped one into his mouth.

You will not talk like that to us, his dad wrote, shaking the page for emphasis.

"Then don't act like I'm not in the room when I am." He continued eating until his dad put a hand on his shoulder. "It's hurtful, Dad." Scott waited for the touch to grow stronger, but it gentled. "I know you're worried, but how about trying to worry about the things I'm worried about? I was scared about the accident and what happened, but now I know. Marshall actually hit me on purpose. I can either freak out about that—and I probably will eventually—or I can be relieved because I know what happened. I'm not in the dark. I have some answers." He turned around. "And I found out something else." Scott pulled out the chair next to him, and his dad sat down. "I learned today that Brent loves me. I mean, really loves me."

"How?" his dad asked.

"You should have seen his face. When Marshall had me, the look in Brent's eyes—it was pain combined with determination. He flew at him and took him out like that." He snapped his fingers. "Then as soon as he was under control, all that mattered was me. He was right there." Scott blushed. "Brent made sure I was okay, held me, protected me from the police when one of them started giving me grief. He was like a lion, Dad. No, that's not it. He was protective, like someone taking a bullet for someone else. Do you know what I mean?" He was having a hard time finding the words. "Brent was willing to put himself in danger, in the line of fire, for me."

His dad nodded and grabbed a piece of scrap paper. *I'd do that for both you and your mother.*

"I know you would." Scott handed his dad a strawberry. "You always have. See, that's how I understand love. From watching you and Mom. I know when you care for someone because of the way you treat each other, and now I think I've found someone who will love me the way you love each other." Scott swallowed. "I know Brent was there at the hospital and that he's been there for me these last few weeks, but I kept expecting him to back away. That me not being able to hear was going to turn out to be too much. But I don't think that's true…. At least, I don't think he's going to let me being deaf stop him from loving me."

His dad leaned over and hugged him. Scott was learning that sometimes so much could be said with touch and a hug. He knew exactly what his father was saying to him. He'd heard it so many times when he was growing up. All his mom and dad wanted was for him to be happy and to find someone who loved him as much as they loved each other. Scott knew he truly had found that.

The issue was, how was he going to tell Brent?

Saying he loved someone was one thing, but this was different. He had changed. Words had lost some of their power for him. He needed to be able to tell Brent how he felt without words, and therein lay the rub.

CHAPTER 9

BRENT WAS nervous as all hell—he had been for the past few days. He and Scott had spent most of their free time together, and Brent was loving every second. Scott had taken to spending more nights at Brent's apartment, and thankfully his mom and dad didn't seem to mind. They talked briefly when Brent came to pick up Scott or drop him off. More than once Brent had seen the two of them share expressions of hope between them, and Brent thought, maybe wished, that meant they approved of the two of them being together.

Neither of Scott's parents had said anything about the age difference or the fact that Brent and Scott worked together. Maybe they had grown to accept those things because they weren't an issue for either Brent or Scott. In Brent's mind, those had been things that he and Scott needed to come to terms with, and they had done so. After two years of dancing around each other, something like that shouldn't have been an issue any longer—and wasn't, much to Brent's relief.

"Why do you keep pacing?" James asked as he brought in a tray from the kitchen. James had called and invited Brent to stop by for coffee after work. Scott was spending the evening with his parents. They wanted to take Scott shopping for a new car now that the insurance issues had been taken care of. Brent had wanted to go along as well, but James had called with his invitation. "Trevor says he thinks there's something wrong."

"So instead of asking me, he gets you to invite me over?"

"Of course not." James set down the tray with practiced ease. It was great seeing the way James moved effortlessly through his home, with Penny, his guide dog, right beside him watching his every move. If Brent weren't well aware that James was blind, he would have sworn James could see. But of course he knew it was just familiarity with his environment. "Well, maybe a little. He says you've been preoccupied and it hasn't been about work. So I thought it might have been about Scott. Are you worried about him and his challenges?"

Brent shook his head and realized he was making gestures to a blind man. "No. It isn't that. I asked Trevor about that once. He told me he loved you for you and the rest didn't matter. I think that's how I feel for Scott. I love him. I think I have in some way since the first day I showed up at the garage and he approached Trevor and me, asking if he was going to still have a job, because Alan the thief had hired him and he was afraid that we'd think he was tainted or something. Even as scared as he was then, there was a kind of fire behind his eyes, and dammit if he didn't keep looking at me. And every time he did, that fire lit something in me… for two years, and I did nothing about it." Brent conked himself on the side of the head. Again, a gesture to a blind man. He really needed to get his head screwed on straight.

"Then what is it?" James sat down, and Penny curled up at his feet. She was an amazing dog, and even when she wasn't in her harness, her devotion to James was amazing. James motioned toward the chair. "Just sit before you make me dizzy."

"How can I?" Brent asked out of curiosity as he moved to where James indicated.

"I keep trying to follow your voice, but it's in a different spot all the time. You can see, so you follow visual cues. I use auditory ones, but the effect is the same." He waited until Brent lowered himself into the chair. "So spill. What's going on?"

"All right. I'm trying to think of a way to say something important to Scott, but I'm not going to just write the words on a sheet of paper and give it to him. There has to be a better way, a more significant way, for me to tell him what I want." Brent sighed and took a cup of coffee off the tray, and James did the same. "I mean...."

"You want to tell Scott how much you care for him?" James seemed amused and smiled behind his mug, eyes twinkling like some mischievous elf.

"Yes. It's important that I do it right, and I want it to be memorable and meaningful... and, God, not lame or stupid." Brent hesitated as his stomach churned, and he set the mug back on the tray. "I know that Scott keeps wondering when I'm going to walk away. I can see it in his eyes whenever he gets super quiet and doesn't think I'm watching as he looks at me. He gets these little lines around his mouth that he only does when he's worried about something."

James sipped his coffee once again but didn't say anything, which was annoying. James almost always had ideas about things like this. Trevor was the action kind of guy, but James was thoughtful and usually had really good ideas. He and Trevor made one hell of a team.

"Okay. I think what you're saying is that you want a way to tell Scott something important, and you want it to be in a way that tells him how you feel, but also that you love him and that the fact that he's deaf doesn't matter. That you love him in spite of his deafness?"

Brent scowled and might have growled. "Does Trevor love you in spite of your blindness, or does he just love you because you're you and you happen to be blind?"

James smiled, and Brent got this idea that he'd just passed some sort of test. He scowled again, but a fat lot of good it did him. "Okay. I understand where you're coming from and I think that maybe I might have an idea. Let me make a few phone calls. What I have in mind I can't directly help you with, but I know someone who can," James said.

Brent picked up his mug once again, wondering at the gleam in James's eyes. He might not have been able to see, but

James was quite expressive at times. "Do you intend to tell me what this grand idea is, or am I going to be kept in the dark?"

James chuckled. "Since I'm in the dark permanently, I don't think it's going to hurt *you* to wait a day or so."

"Cute. The blind guy is making blind jokes." Brent sat back.

"Why not? I do it better than anyone else. I also tell great deaf jokes. Did you hear the one about the blind guy and the deaf guy?"

"No."

"Neither did the deaf guy." James kept a straight face as Brent looked up at the ceiling.

"That's really awful." Brent groaned softly. "You should put together an act."

Penny lifted her head and snuffled as though she were giving her opinion on the idea.

"What she said," James echoed, gently stroking her head. "You're my best girl, aren't you? You know—and I'm jumping ahead here—when you get a place together, you should get Scott a dog."

Brent wondered if James had gone nuts for a second.

"A service dog. Not one like Penny, but one that's been trained to work with the deaf. They're trained to alert their owners to sounds like the doorbell, timers, or even a person calling their name."

That wasn't a bad idea. Brent wondered where he'd go for something like that. He'd have to find out. "Anyway, this idea of yours?"

James huffed. "You're like a dog with a bone, aren't you? Let me make a few calls tomorrow and I'll see what I can do." James grinned and then leaned forward, finally telling Brent what he had in mind. It was a great idea—perfect, in fact—and Brent wished to hell he'd come up with it. "I'll call you with the details if he agrees."

"DON'T YOU need to go to work today?" Scott asked when Brent came over on Saturday morning. Brent had arranged for

Scott to have the day off on the pretext that he wasn't supposed to be working full hours yet. He had also arranged for Darryl to watch over the shop for the day.

Nope, I took a vacation day. Trevor is going to stop in to check on things at some point, but I have everything set, and Darryl knows what to do. It will be fine. Brent was so excited, but he tried not to let it show on his face. *Do you want to do something?* God, being cagey was a pain in the ass. *I have an idea, if you're up for it.*

"Sure. I think I'm driving Mom crazy. She keeps hovering around me and watching me like I'm going to break or something. I know she's trying to tell me something without actually telling me."

Your mom is worried, and you can't blame her. She nearly lost you, just like the rest of us, and it scared her. Give her a break and some time. He knew almost exactly how she felt. *Let's go.*

Carolyn came into the room, and Brent waved to her before Scott went outside to wait for him. Brent hurried to the car and pulled away.

"What was that?" Scott asked.

Brent flashed his most innocent smile.

"I saw you give my mom a thumbs-up. Are you two in league about something?" Scott narrowed his eyes, but Brent couldn't write a note, so he shrugged and continued driving. "Where are we going? What's in Whitefish Bay?"

Brent patted Scott's knee and headed toward James and Trevor's house.

"Are we going to see James?" Scott sounded excited as they got out of the car. James opened the door as they approached, and Penny came out to greet both of them before doing her business and then going back inside to be near James.

James motioned them inside to where a young lady stood waiting for them. "I'm Grace Hormel," she said as she signed slowly. Brent turned to Scott, who watched her fingers with rapt fascination. Then she handed Scott an index card and let him read it as she continued on. "I teach at the School for the Deaf. I am able to hear now, but spent most of my life without being able to." She turned and pulled back her hair. Small devices were attached to her head behind the ear. Cochlear implants. "These allow me to hear now, but I understand you aren't a candidate." She wrote a note to Scott as she spoke.

Scott shook his head. "My brain was injured in an accident. They tell me that my ears and even most of the nerves to the brain are fine, but my brain isn't and I lost my hearing. They tell me it was unusual, but it's what happened."

She nodded and wrote again as she talked. This was a skill she must have mastered in her teaching. "I'm here today because James contacted us with a special request from your boyfriend." She glanced at Brent as she spoke and handed Scott the page. "We're going to work on some basic signing today. I know you've both registered for classes, and I look forward to working with you." She placed the pad on the table and motioned for both of them to sit down on the sofa. She sat in the chair across the way. James took the other chair, and Penny sat next to him, her head on his lap.

Grace opened a bag that rested beside the chair and pulled out a tablet. She worked with it a minute and started up a video, placing it where they could see it. It was a brief introduction. Then she brought up a blank Word document.

"I thought I'd start with some basic signs so you both can get started and say some simple things to each other. American Sign Language is a complete language, but instead of spoken words, it uses hand gestures. There are nuances and regional and individual differences, just like with spoken language. Most people don't think about it, but when I first got the implants and was able to hear, I had to learn what actual spoken English sounded like and what it meant. See, to me, this was *house*." She paused and used her hands to make the sign. "Not the spoken word, which I had never heard," she added as she typed again. "You will learn the basics of the language in your classes. I'm here just to get you started."

"Is that okay?" Brent asked after turning to Scott so he could see him.

"I can't believe you did all this for me." Scott's voice broke a little. He blinked and then turned away.

Brent patted his hand, waiting for him to turn back, nodded, and pointed to James. Brent took the pad on the table. *I wanted to be able to talk to you again, and I thought this would be a way to get started. We have a week or so until class, but James suggested this might be good for both of us.*

Scott hugged him so tightly Brent was afraid he wasn't going to be able to breathe, but it really didn't matter. Compared to the happy shine in Scott's eyes, air was overrated.

"Are you ready to get started?" Grace asked when Scott released him, and they both nodded. Grace started with simple words and ideas and how to convey them—*I, you, we,* and so on. "In class you will learn the alphabet and other basics, so I want to help you express some common ideas," she went on to explain, then showed them the hand signs for *hungry* and *tired* before combining them with others.

"I am hungry," she typed on the screen and then slowly made the gestures as they both followed along. Then Grace continued, explaining some more and then showing them how to put them together. It took Brent a few tries, but he was able to get the hang of it. Scott learned quickly and it took him less practice than Brent, but they were both able to make the motions.

After a few hours, they had learned enough to make some simple sentences. What surprised Brent was how much concentration it took for him to make the sign instead of or in conjunction with talking. Talking was so natural that it took extra effort not to.

They thanked Grace once they were done. "You both did very well," she signed and spoke. Scott smiled and gave her a hug. In a way, it had to be like unlocking a part of him now. Just like that, Scott had another way to receive information. Granted, it was still limited for now, but after not too long, it was going to open worlds for him.

Scott excused himself to go to the bathroom, and Brent took advantage of his absence. "Please show me one more sign," he asked, then told her what he wanted, checking that Scott was gone. Grace smiled and carefully showed him what he wanted to know.

"I think I'll let you teach that one to Scott," she said with a wink.

"Thank you." Brent shook her hand and walked her to the door. James followed with Penny, and he hugged Grace and thanked her as well.

"Sign language is helpful to those who are deaf, but it has one big drawback: most people you meet during the day don't know how to speak it. A lot of deaf people tend to spend their time with other hearing-impaired people because it's easy for them to communicate. For you and those closest to him, learning ASL is great, but things like lip-reading and other techniques are important as well. He has a ways to go, and it can be frustrating. Know that and expect it. It takes plenty of support to learn a whole new way to interact with the world."

Brent nodded his understanding, thanking her once again. He also thanked James for all his help and knelt down to give Penny some attention, until Scott came back. Once Scott joined them again, they said goodbye to Grace. She told them both that she looked forward to seeing them in class and that they were off to a good start. She also pointed them to some good websites and resource materials before leaving the house.

Brent and Scott got ready to leave as well, because James needed to change and get ready for lunch. Apparently Trevor was stopping back on the motorcycle to pick him up, and James was almost too excited to stand still for very long. They said goodbye, sharing hugs.

"I appreciate this so much," Brent told James.

"You're welcome." James squeezed him, and then let Brent go.

Brent and Scott returned to the car and pulled away as Trevor passed them going the other way, completely badass on his Harley in his black leathers. James was in for one hell of a ride, from the look of it.

"Are we going anywhere else?" Scott asked, his eyes wide and his cheeks a little flushed. "That was a great surprise." Sometimes Scott blew him away with his energy and the way he didn't let things get him down.

Brent nodded, returning his smile, glancing at Scott as he practiced his symbols while he rode. It wasn't far for Brent to drive, and he pulled into the park. As soon as Scott saw where they were, his smile told Brent he knew where they were heading.

The sun was burning, but the relief was instant as they stepped under the trees, the sound of the water pulling them both forward to the little creek and its gently turning waterwheel. Their bench was empty, and Brent sat next to Scott.

"Thank you for doing that. I was nervous, wondering if I would be good at signing. But we did well." Scott bumped him. *Pretty water*, he signed.

Yes, Brent signed back, then turned to Scott, touching his hands gently to quiet him. He made the sign Grace taught him. Then Brent signed the entire phrase. *I love you.* He waited and did it again, mouthing the words. *I love you.*

Scott gasped, then gave a brilliant smile.

I love you.

"Did you do that so you could say that to me? Is that why Grace came over?" Scott asked, copying the signs Brent made.

Yes. Brent ran out of signs and had to resort to pen and paper. He handed Scott the note and let him read it. *I wanted to tell you how I felt in a way that was special.* Then Brent touched his chin so Scott looked at him again. *I love you,* he signed yet again, then took Scott's hands and placed them over his heart. "I love you." He pulled Scott to him and held him tight.

"I love you too," Scott said into his ear. "I've been in love with you for a long time, but I didn't say anything because you were my boss, and then after the accident.... I can't figure out how you could fall in love with a deaf guy."

Brent took Scott's arms, unwrapping them so Scott sat back from him. *I didn't fall for someone deaf,* he scrawled in the book. *I fell for you.* He made the sign for *you* that Grace had taught them. Scott was funny and smart, cute, hot, sexy, brave, stubborn, and so many other things. But mostly Scott was his. *You, me,* he signed, then brought their hands together, hoping Scott would understand.

Scott smiled and leaned in to bring their lips together in a kiss so hot that if they were any closer to the stream, they'd be surrounded by clouds of steam. Beads of sweat burst out on Brent's forehead, but he didn't care at all. Scott could make his blood boil and his temperature rise just by looking at him. One kiss was stratospheric.

Brent wished he could tell Scott all the things he wanted to, but he wasn't going to write another damned note, so he let his lips do the talking. That turned out to be a much better idea, judging by the soft whimpers Scott made deep in his throat.

The sound of footsteps crunching old leaves underfoot made Brent pull away, but they shared smiles and heated looks that promised so much once they were alone.

A black-haired man who was chiseled-jaw handsome approached the clearing, holding the hand of a blond boy of about five. The boy ran to the water's edge, just seconds from stepping in. "Can I play, Daddy?"

The man sat on the bench next to Scott, waved his son over, and helped him take off his shoes, then let him play in the few inches of water that turned the wheel. The boy laughed, splashed, and held the wheel still, then released it with a whoosh of water, giggling. Brent leaned against Scott as the boy did it again, laughing out loud as he played with the water.

"We always come here," the man said, with a smile that looked forced. "This is his favorite spot." There was pain behind his eyes. "This is one of the few times he's laughed like this since his mother died a few months ago. He asks all the time if he can play with the wheel."

"I love it too." He watched them, knowing how it felt to lose someone so precious. In a way, watching the boy play, it was like his dad was helping, even now.

Brent slipped his arm around Scott's waist as a wave of contentment washed over him. He was here with Scott, who had ultimately helped erase some of the guilt and pain of his father's death. Brent wasn't a coward, he knew that now, though he'd likely still have repercussions to work through. And the more he thought about it, the more he figured his dad would hate for him to feel that way. His dad would want him to be happy. Now he truly was, especially with Scott next to him.

"My dad fixed it some years ago. The original had broken, so he rebuilt it." Brent tugged Scott a little closer. "He was a Milwaukee Police detective and was killed protecting me when I was a kid. I've come here for years to be closer to him." Brent smiled.

"I'm sorry," the man said, turning back to his son, who continued playing and nearly fell in the water. Not that it was going to make much difference in how wet the little guy got.

"Don't be. My dad would be thrilled to see how happy your son is." And that was so true.

Brent used to come here because his dad made the wheel and he felt closer to him. Yeah, and maybe because of the guilt he carried. He'd looked for answers here, though there were none to be had. Now he would come here because it was where he and Scott had finally confessed their love. From now on that was what he was going to remember about this place. His dad would be so pleased.

"You guys have fun." Brent stood, and Scott did the same. Then Brent took Scott's hand, threaded their fingers together, and started down the path. It was time to leave his past behind and take hold of his future, their future... together.

EPILOGUE

I GOT the last box, Brent signed before going out to retrieve the rest of Scott's things from Dean's truck. There hadn't been a lot of stuff, since Scott was moving in from his parents', although they'd had to pick one of the coldest and windiest days of January to make the move. They had decided to try to find a house to rent, and one near Trevor and James had become available, so Brent had arranged for it and moved in before the holidays and gotten things settled. Now Scott was joining him, making the house a home, just like that.

Okay. I unpack, Scott signed in return. Sometimes they didn't always make the right signs, or messed them up, but they were able to communicate simpler ideas and phrases using their hands. It was taking time, but after their first course, they had made progress, Scott more than him. That was okay, though. They used it every day as much as possible and often looked up signs so they could build their vocabulary. It was becoming easier and more natural by the day.

Brent was well aware that learning and being fluent were going to take time—a lot of time—but they helped each other, and with Scott's parents taking classes as well, Scott's world seemed to be opening up once again, rather than contracting. That made Brent happy because Scott was happier.

Brent pulled his coat closer around him and went outside, stood against the wind as he got to the truck parked out front, and retrieved the final box. Snow swirled around his feet as he trudged back up the walk and inside, then shoved the door closed to block out the cold. He set the box on the hall floor and took off his gloves, thankful to be warm and dry.

"Is that it?" Scott hurried in, glancing at the box and then carrying it away toward the stairs. "We won't need this until the holidays next year."

Brent pulled off his coat and went out back to shake off the snow in the mudroom, and then hung it up. As Brent unloaded, Scott had been putting things away so the house wasn't cluttered with boxes and things. Brent checked the time and glanced out the windows to where the light was already fading on one of the shortest days of the year. He had brought in some wood, so he laid a fire and let it take off the last of the chill. He closed the screen as the flames caught and the wood crackled and popped on the grate.

"This looks like something from a greeting card," Scott said as he entered the room and sat in one of the comfortable chairs near the fire. "I'm cold."

Brent snorted, grateful Scott couldn't hear him. He set down the poker, turning to Scott. *I was the one out in the cold*, he signed, or hoped he did.

Scott shrugged. "I'm still cold."

Brent added another log to the growing fire, closed the screen again, and sat on the sofa. *It will warm up soon.* He loved this. The wind whistled around the corners of the house, and yet they were warm. Brent was as content as he could ever remember being… until the lights flickered and went out. The house went silent, with the fan on the furnace stopping as well. That meant that even though the furnace was gas, there would only be the fireplace for heat until the power came back on.

He motioned for Scott to stay still, went to the kitchen to retrieve two flashlights, and brought one to Scott. Then Brent returned to the kitchen, used a match to light one of the burners, and opened the refrigerator. He removed a container of soup his mom had made, grabbed a couple of beers as well, and closed the door quickly, then transferred the soup to a pan to warm through. Brent got some crackers, brought them into the living room, and set them on the coffee table. Then he did the same with the beer, and once the soup was heated, brought that in as well, in two bowls. He and Scott sat in front of the flickering fire, eating warm soup, watching the dancing flames. It was quiet, settling, and incredibly domestic.

They ate without talking, which had become quite normal, their hands otherwise occupied. Over time, their mouths and lips would be used primarily for other things, special things, especially when they were alone. Brent took care of the dishes when they were finished, then hurried upstairs and returned with a couple of blankets that he laid out on the sofa, and they curled together once Scott added more wood to the fire.

"Is your mom okay?" Scott asked when Brent's phone lit up on the coffee table with a message.

Brent nodded. She was at Mike's, and apparently they were battened down to wait out the power outage for the evening. His mom was as happy as Brent could remember her being. It seemed they had both finally managed to move past the loss of his dad and the aftermath of the events of that day. *We're good here*, he returned. *Stay warm.*

Brent sent quick messages to Dean and Trevor just to make sure they were all safe and sound. A message came quickly from Trevor that he and James were hunkered down and still had power. Dean didn't respond right away, but when he did, Brent showed Scott the message.

My power is out too. I was going to go out, but am staying at home, huddled under blankets.

"We have to find him someone special. He deserves it," Scott told him.

Brent smiled. *He does, but for God's sake, we can't play matchmaker*, Brent signed as best he could. He ended up spelling out the last word.

"No way. Though he needs to find someone better than the guys he meets at the club." Scott squirmed until he got comfortable with his back against Brent's chest and his head resting on Brent's shoulder, body throwing off heat like a furnace. Brent leaned forward, and Scott turned around a little, just enough that he was able to reach his lips. Their kiss was gentle, but heated quickly, Brent holding Scott more tightly. "What are you doing?" Scott stilled, turning to look into Brent's eyes.

"Nothing."

"No. That wasn't nothing. You were signing—I could feel it against my back. You do that sometimes."

"I guess so." Brent leaned forward again, but Scott pulled away, and Brent let him go, bringing his hands around to the front so Scott could see them. Certain ideas and thoughts seemed to flow not from his brain to his mouth, but from his mind directly to his fingers. Brent signed, and Scott smiled slightly.

I love you too, Scott signed in return and then placed his hands in the center of Brent's chest. "Is that what you sign against me?"

Brent nodded, then rubbed the back of his neck, trying to think of the best way to explain, but Scott lunged and then his arms were full and explanations seemed completely unnecessary as Scott tugged his shirt up and disappeared under the blankets, his lips finding a nipple, surrounding it in heat and love just briefly before his cheek settled against Brent's chest.

Brent ran his hands along Scott's arm, their warmth blending and building. He gently tapped Scott on the shoulder until he looked up at him. Brent pulled his hands and Scott's head out from under the covers, silhouetting them against the fire. *Will you marry me?*

Scott didn't answer, and Brent made the signs again, carefully, slowly. He had to spell out "marry," but that was okay. Judging by the way Scott's smile warmed the room and sank straight to Brent's heart, he understood.

"Yes," Scott told him. "Yes, most definitely yes."

In that instant, keeping warm was so much less important, and their evening by the fire, in the dark with the power out, turned into a celebration that generated plenty of heat of a different kind, searing the moment into their memories forever. And this time Brent wasn't the only one proving that one didn't need spoken words to touch someone's heart.

ANDREW GREY grew up in western Michigan with a father who loved to tell stories and a mother who loved to read them. Since then he has lived all over the country and traveled throughout the world. He has a master's degree from the University of Wisconsin-Milwaukee and now works full-time on his writing. Andrew received the RWA Centennial Award in 2017. His hobbies include collecting antiques, gardening, and leaving his dirty dishes anywhere but in the sink (particularly when writing). He considers himself blessed with an accepting family, fantastic friends, and the world's most supportive and loving husband. Andrew currently lives in beautiful historic Carlisle, Pennsylvania.

Email: andrewgrey@comcast.net
Website: www.andrewgreybooks.com

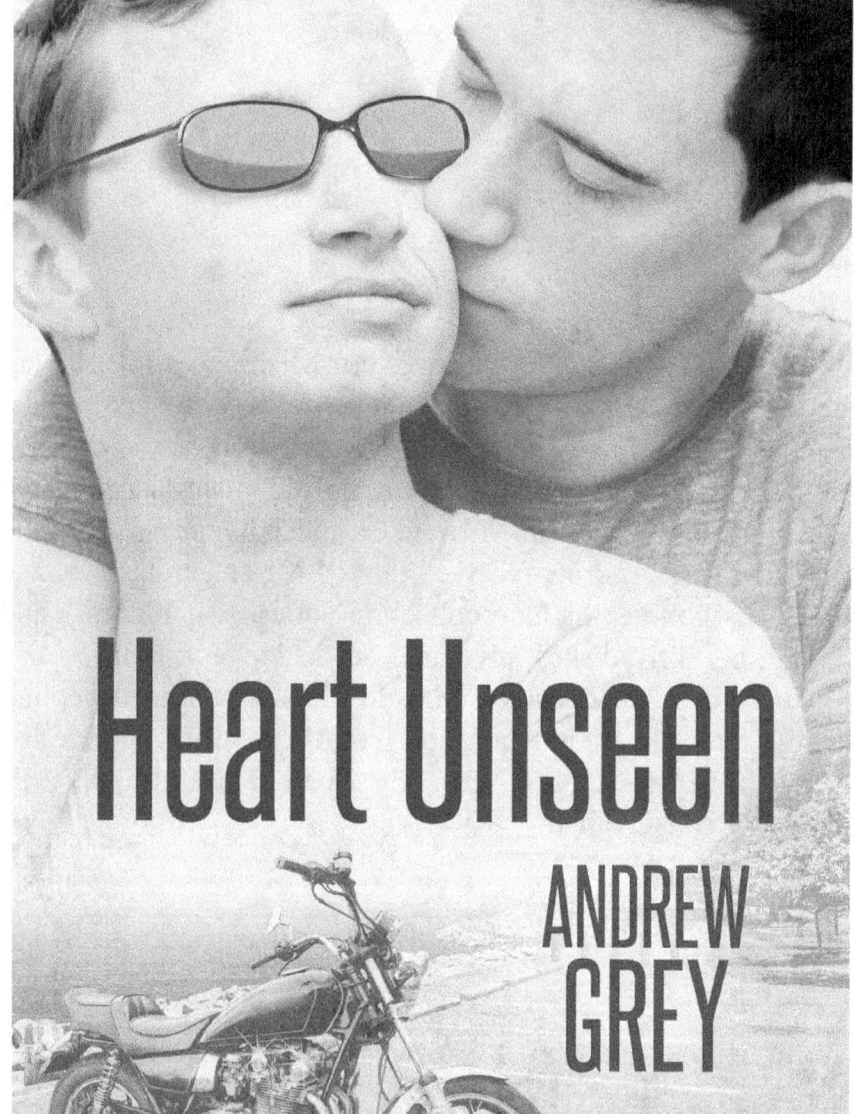

Heart Unseen

ANDREW GREY

A Hearts Entwined Novel

As a stunningly attractive man and the owner of a successful chain of auto repair garages, Trevor is used to attention, adoration, and getting what he wants. What he wants tends to be passionate, no-strings-attached flings with men he meets in clubs. He doesn't expect anything different when he sets his sights on James. Imagine his surprise when the charm that normally brings men to their knees fails to impress. Trevor will need to drop the routine and connect with James on a meaningful level. He starts by offering to take James home instead of James riding home with his intoxicated friend.

For James, losing his sight at a young age meant limited opportunities for social interaction. Spending most of his time working at a school for the blind has left him unfamiliar with Trevor's world, but James has fought hard for his independence, and he knows what he wants. Right now, that means stepping outside his comfort zone and into Trevor's heart.

Trevor is also open to exploring real love and commitment for a change, but before he can be the man James needs him to be, he'll have to deal with the pain of his past.

www.dreamspinnerpress.com

SETTING
the HOOK
ANDREW GREY

Love's Charter: Book One

It could be the catch of a lifetime.

William Westmoreland escapes his unfulfilling Rhode Island existence by traveling to Florida twice a year and chartering Mike Jansen's fishing boat to take him out on the Gulf. The crystal-blue water and tropical scenery isn't the only view William enjoys, but he's never made his move. A vacation romance just isn't on his horizon.

Mike started his Apalachicola charter fishing service as a way to care for his daughter and mother, putting their safety and security ahead of the needs of his own heart. Denying his attraction becomes harder with each of William's visits.

William and Mike's latest fishing excursion starts with a beautiful day, but a hurricane's erratic course changes everything, stranding William. As the wind and rain rage outside, the passion the two men have been trying to resist for years crashes over them. In the storm's wake, it leaves both men yearning to prolong what they have found. But real life pulls William back to his obligations. Can they find a way to reduce the distance between them and discover a place where their souls can meet? The journey will require rough sailing, but the bright future at the end might be worth the choppy seas.

www.dreamspinnerpress.com

TAMING THE BEAST

ANDREW GREY

The suspicious death of Dante Bartholomew's wife changed him, especially in the eyes of the residents of St. Giles. They no longer see a successful businessman… only a monster they believe was involved. Dante's horrific reputation eclipses the truth to the point that he sees no choice but to isolate himself and his heart.

The plan backfires when he meets counselor Beau Clarity and the children he works with. Beau and the kids see beyond the beastly reputation to the beautiful soul inside Dante, and Dante's cold heart begins to thaw as they slip past his defenses. The warmth and hope Beau brings to Dante's life help him see his entire existence—his trials and sorrows—in a brighter light.

But Dante's secrets could rip happiness from their grasp… especially since someone isn't above hurting those Dante has grown to love in order to bring him down.

www.dreamspinnerpress.com

CAN'T LIVE
WITHOUT YOU

ANDREW
GREY

Forever Yours: Book One

Justin Hawthorne worked hard to realize his silver-screen dreams, making his way from small-town Pennsylvania to Hollywood and success. But it hasn't come without sacrifice. When Justin's father kicked him out for being gay, George Miller's family offered to take him in, but circumstances prevented it. Now Justin is back in town and has come face to face with George, the man he left without so much as a good-bye… and the man he's never stopped loving.

Justin's disappearance hit George hard, but he's made a life for himself as a home nurse and finds fulfillment in helping others. When he sees Justin again, George realizes the hole in his heart never mended, and he isn't the only one in need of healing. Justin needs time out of the public eye to find himself again, and George and his mother cannot turn him away. As they stay together in George's home, old feelings are rekindled. Is a second chance possible when everything George cares about is in Pennsylvania and Justin must return to his career in California? First they'll have to deal with the reason for Justin's abrupt departure all those years ago.

www.dreamspinnerprss.com

NEVER LET YOU GO

ANDREW GREY

Sequel to *Can't Live Without You*
Forever Yours: Book Two

Friends since they met in school, Ashton and Brighton soon become much more. Ash and his aunt are Brighton's haven away from his mess of a family, and when Ash enlists in the Army, Brighton learns to endure his long absences and eagerly awaits his return from missions.

Until one day Ash doesn't come back, and Brighton thinks his greatest fear has come true.

Months pass and Brighton grieves for Ash, not knowing that a terrible misunderstanding sent Ash running, unable to cope when he thought Brighton had betrayed him. Even after an emotional reunion, their relationship isn't the same—Brighton is now responsible for his young niece, and he's having a hard time rediscovering the trust he once had in Ash. Ash must still tend to his mental health, but before he can, he'll have to deal with a past secret that puts all their lives at risk. With so many forces determined to tear them apart, can Brighton and Ash hold on to each other and never let go?

www.dreamspinnerpress.com

www.ingramcontent.com/pod-product-compliance
Lightning Source LLC
Chambersburg PA
CBHW060059260626
47160CB00005B/1722